THE LYONESSE STONE

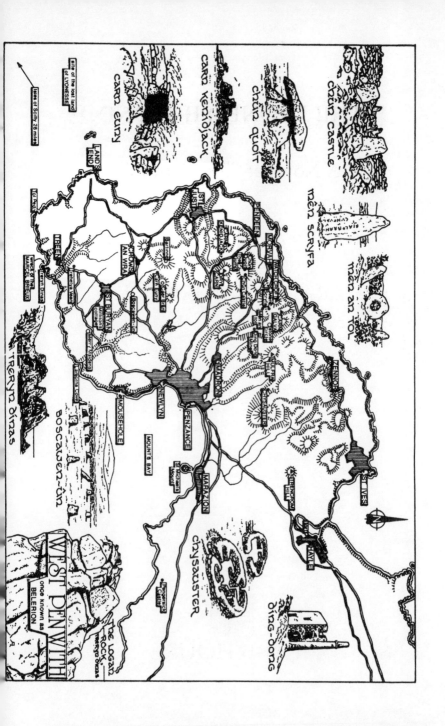

THE LYONESSE STONE

A Novel of West Cornwall

by

CRAIG WEATHERHILL

Illustrated by

The Author

TABB HOUSE

First published 1991
Tabb House, 7 Church Street, Padstow, Cornwall, PL28 8BG

ISBN 0 907018 85 8

Hardback edition ISBN 0 907018 90 4

Typeset by Exe Valley Dataset, Exeter
Printed by Bookcraft (Bath) Ltd, Midsomer Norton, Bath

CONTENTS

LIST OF ILLUSTRATIONS

AUTHOR'S NOTE

I OWE the tale of *The Lyonesse Stone* to the ancient and magnificently rich legendary heritage of West Cornwall, as it is firmly founded on a number of its countless legends, and to those nineteenth-century worthies who snatched that heritage back from the jaws of obscurity. In particular, these were William Bottrell, the 'Old Celt', whose three volumes of *Traditions and Hearthside Stories of West Cornwall* were published between 1870 and 1880, Robert Hunt, whose *Popular Romances of the West of England* first appeared in 1881; and Margaret Courtney, with her *Cornish Feasts and Folk-Lore (1890)*.

The legend of the destruction of the Lyonesse, in the form in which it appears in this book, is all but forgotten, being totally missed by most authors on the subject, including Bottrell, Hunt and Courtney, and modern Arthurian scholars, since its inclusion in *Scilly and its Legends* by the Rev. H. J. Whitfeld in 1852. This is the only story to assert that Medraut (Sir Mordred) survived Arthur's last battle at Camlann, and it is a valuable legend for that fact alone.

I have also wanted to demonstrate that the legendary heritage of Cornwall is an entity of tremendous quality and power which has not deserved the distortion and trivialisation it has suffered at the hands of the tourist trade and which has only served to undo the valuable work of Bottrell, Hunt, Courtney and the Federation of Old Cornwall Societies.

My thanks must go to those who have advised and encouraged me in the writing of this book: notably Mr and Mrs P. A. S. Pool of Treeve, Connor Downs; the late Nigel Tangye of Glendorgal, Newquay; David Clarke of Four Lanes; Hugh Miners of Penzance, and others too numerous to list. I owe a further debt of gratitude to Gorseth Byrth Kernow: the Gorsedd of the Bards of Cornwall, for kindly allowing me to reproduce extracts from the modern Gorsedd ceremony.

With the necessary exception of Trehelya Vean (and the Lyonesse), every location in *The Lyonesse Stone* actually exists as described. My characters are, of course, fictitious, but the Trevelyan family is a large, scattered and ancient clan whose coat-of-arms is just as described in the first chapter.

There is, today, no custodian at the Carn Euny Ancient Monument, but I will apologise to those custodians of the past, none of whom resembled in any way the character I have portrayed. My apologies also to the Rector of St Buryan and his predecessors, none of whom is the unfortunate priest of the early chapters.

The characters of the Lord of Pengersek and Jack of the Hammer are drawn straight from legend, and I saw no reason to alter them except for the most minor details. The same applies also to Pengersek's demon-mare, although I have given her a name. A footnote to Robert Hunt's collection, comparing the characters of Jack and Weland the Smith, gave me the idea of actually blending the two. The spriggans are legendary creatures peculiar to West Penwith, but not generally as vicious as I have portrayed them.

Corantyn and Gawen are not legendary characters as such, but were adapted from tales of the Small People, especially those which are said to inhabit the headland and Iron Age fort of Treryn Dinas, which also has connections with Arthur and Merlin. Merlin himself is said to have uttered a number of local prophecies: I merely invented yet another. The Nôshelyas are my invention in name only, for they are loosely based on local variants of the Wild Hunt; one of Carn Kenidjack's hair-raising legends; and on aspects of the Lord of Pengersek himself.

Railobran and Selus were real people of the sixth century and their inscribed memorial stones can still be seen as described within these pages. Selus, or Selyf, is thought by some to have been the son of King Gerent of Cornwall and the brother of St Just. After his days as a warrior, he too became a holy man, St Seleven (St Levan).

All the Celtic personal names are genuine, some being drawn from local place-names: Sulyan and Gwythno being from the adjacent farms of Nanjulian and Nanquidno (Sulyan's valley; Gwythno's valley). The farm of Tregiffian (Gyfyan's farm) stands nearby. Similarly, Sylvestre, chieftain of Chysauster, comes from the earliest known form of that name: Chysalvestre (House of Sylvestre).

The name Belerion should also be explained. It does not appear on modern maps, but it is the oldest known name of the Land's End peninsula, a native Celtic name which was recorded in the fourth century BC by a Greek explorer and still used four hundred years later by Ptolemy. It is not known when it fell out of use.

The place-names of West Cornwall are mostly Celtic and seldom pronounced quite as they appear. The placing of emphasis differs from most English names; for example, in two-syllable words, the stress is often on the second syllable, so we have PenZANCE, not PENzance. In words of three or more syllables, it is usually the penultimate one which is stressed, e.g. PenGERsek.

The following list is of some of the names found in this book; how they are pronounced and, where known, what they mean.

BARTINNÊ,	bar-TIN-ee	Hill of fires
BARTINNEY		
BELERION	bel-EH-ree-an	The Shining One
BODINNAR	bod-IN-er	Fortified homestead
BOSCAWEN-ÛN	bs-cow-NOON	Dwelling by an elder tree on the downs
CAER BRÂN	care BRAYN	Fort Crow
CAER TRYGVA	care TRIG-va	Fort by a townplace
CARN EUNY	carn YOO-nee	St Euny's tor
CARN KENIDJACK	carn kn-IJ-ek	Hooting tor
CHÛN	choon	House on the downs
CHYSAUSTER	chez-OY-ster	House of Sylvestre
CORANTYN	caw-RAN-tin	Elf of the castle;
NADELEK	nad-EL-ek	Christmas
CROWS-AN-WRA	crowz (rhymes with cows) an-RAY	The witch's cross
DAGRENOU	dag-REN-a	Tears
FOGOU	FOO-goo	Cave
GAWEN	GAOU-en	Meaning not known
GORHEDER	gor-HED-er	Very bold
GÛNAJYNYAL	goon-aj-IN-yal	Downs of the desolate gap
GWYTHNO	GWITH-no	Battle-known

GWYTHYAS HOWLSEDHAS	GWITH-yas howl-SETH-az	Guardian of the West
LETHOWSA	leth-OW-za	The Milky Ones (old name of the Seven Stones)
LOGAN	LOGG-an	Rocking (dialect word)
LYONESSE	lee-an-EZ	Meaning not known
MARGHAS-VYGHAN	Mar-haz VEE-han	Little market (Marazion)
NÔSHELYAS	nawz-HEL-yaz	Night hunters
PENDEEN	pn-DEEN	Fortified headland
PENGERSEK	pen-GER-zik (hard G)	Marsh end
PENWITH	pen-WITH	Furthest end
PENZANCE	pn-ZANCE	Holy headland
PORTHCURNO	porth-KER-no	Cove of headlands
RIALOBRAN	ree-AL-o-brayn	Royal Raven
ST BURYAN	BURR-yan	St Beriana
SENNEN	SEN-an	St Senan
SPRIGGAN	SPRID-jan	Spirit, goblin
TARANWYN	tah-ran-WIN	White thunder
TOL-PEDN-PENWITH	tol-pedn-pen-WITH	Holed headland at the furthest end
TREHELYA VEAN	tre-HEL-ya VEE-an	Lesser Hunter's Farm
TREHELYA VEOR	tre-HEL-ya VEER	Greater Hunter's Farm
TREHYLLYS	TRIL-IZ	Farm by an old stronghold
TRERYN DINAS	treen DIN-us	Castle of the fortress town
TREVELYAN	tre-VEL-yan	Milvan's farm
TREVYLYAN	tre-VIL-yan	Milvan's farm
WOON GUMPUS (The Gump)	Woon GUMP-az	Level downs

I have watered down the dialect and accent of West Penwith a little reluctantly, but had I reproduced it in its broadest form, it might have been incomprehensible to many. I hope the purists will forgive me, and also the archaeologists, as I have taken one or two small liberties.

Craig Weatherhill

Bard DELYNYER HENDHYSOANS of the Gorsedd of Cornwall

Penwith, Kernow: 1990

THO: An Cove rag
WELLA BOTTRELL: An Celt Coath
(1816–1881)

PART ONE

THE CROWNSTONE

1: TREHELYA VEAN

THE summer storm had been born in mid-Atlantic. Gathering speed and venom, it moved threateningly north-eastward until finally confronting the formidable barrier of the Land's End cliffs.

The result was totally unlike anything John and Penny Trevelyan had ever experienced. The wind screamed dementedly across the bleak landscape, striving to pluck buildings from their roots, and even though the old lane wound between high granite hedges, they were forced to stagger against the strength of the gusts.

"Just as well you missed the rain," their uncle shouted above the roar. Ben Trevelyan was a big man, but even he was being battered by the gale. "Like iron rods, 'twas, an' 'orizontal too. Stung like 'ell. Me an' Ned got soaked to the skin gettin' the cows in for milkin'. Not that you'd 'ave noticed. Still sleepin' like babes at nine o'clock."

"Where are we going, Ben?" John shouted back.

"Same place we went yesterday. We won't go out on the headland, though. Too dangerous in this wind. Thought I'd show 'ee a real sea."

THE day before seemed a world away. The first full day of John and Penny's holiday, it had been one of blue skies, unbroken sunshine and light breezes. They had both been born in West Cornwall, but had left at an early age when their father, Ben's younger brother, had taken a position up-country. Now he had been asked to go out to the Middle East for three weeks and their mother had accepted a rare chance to go with him.

Ben had been delighted when asked if John and Penny could stay with him. Despite loyal attention from his ageing farm-hand Ned Hosken, and Ned's wife Nellie, he was a lonely man. His own wife had died just three years before, when only in her early forties, and Ben had never really recovered from the shock. He had no children of his own, and to have such a lively pair around the farm was a tonic to him.

John and Penny had taken to him from the moment he'd met them on the platform of Penzance railway station. Close on fifty, he was a powerful six-footer with a thick crop of curling iron-grey hair, bushy sideburns, and a brown, weather-worn face, crinkled and creased from years of farming on land exposed to fierce Atlantic gales. Dark eyes sparkled with humour and his voice boomed as he chatted freely in the forceful tones of West Cornwall. His knowledge of the area was impressive and he kept them entertained with stories.

Ben's farm, Trehelya Vean, was typical of the area. The granite farmhouse stood four-square to the wild Cornish winters and had shrugged off more than 250 of them. Barns, outbuildings and the Hoskens' cottage, all of the same stone and roofed with cement- washed scantle slate, huddled around it.

Penny, wondering about the strange names that all the local places had, and especially that of the farm itself, had asked Ben about it on the first evening.

"Like most place-names round here," he told them, "tes of the old Cornish language; a Celtic tongue, like Welsh an' Breton, an' thousands o' years old. Trehelya Vean would be Lesser Hunter's Farm in English. There used to be a Trehelya Veor – Greater Hunter's Farm – but tes mostly gone now. There are still some ruins of 'en, four fields over to Penberth side, but tes only bits of overgrown walls in the corner. The old folk won't go near the place. They d'say tes haunted; full o' spriggans an' that, but I've been here all my life an' seen nothin'."

2

All the farm fields had their own names, most of them Cornish. The one with the remains of the earlier farm was Park Crellas: field of the ruin.

The farm stood only three miles from the Land's End itself and to the north, a mile or so away, the high tower of St Buryan church dominated a flat, almost treeless landscape. Not for another two miles in that direction did the land begin to rise to the first of the great moorland hills which formed the granite spine of West Penwith, the Land's End peninsula, stretching north- eastward as far as St Ives.

According to Ben, those windswept heights were crowded with prehistoric remains: stone circles, giant dolmens, standing stones, fortresses and settlements as old as Time itself. It was a place packed with legend, too. Strange, sometimes frightening, tales clustered around the peninsula.

On the following day, Ben had taken them to the nearby headland of Treryn Dinas, a place of many legends. They had never seen a more beautiful or spectacular place. The headland was a series of splintered towers and pinnacles soaring to a height of two hundred feet above the Atlantic rollers that creamed against the base of the granite cliffs and on the sands of Porthcurno and Pednavounder. Here and there, pockets of the greenest turf studded with sea-pinks clung to the rock and plaintive gulls wheeled overhead.

The farmer pointed out the four lines of defence which ran across the headland from cliff to cliff. The landward one was huge: an earth rampart some twenty feet high. These, he told them, had been built two-and-a-half thousand years ago by the Celtic population and was one of the finest Iron Age cliff castles in Cornwall. Legend, though, said that the giants had built the fortifications and there were many stories of them. The Small People, a beautiful faery race, were still said to inhabit the place and tend the gardens of flowers on inaccessible ledges. King Arthur had been here, and Merlin too.

On this headland was one of the natural wonders of Cornwall: a seventy-ton rock perched on a high crag and so finely balanced that even John, to his delight, found that he could make the huge boulder rock ponderously. It was called the Logan Rock,

"Loggan, not lowgan," said Ben. "Loggin' means rocking or swaying."

Once, he told them, it could be rocked by the wind, but in 1824 Lieutenant Goldsmith and the crew of HMS *Nimble* had toppled it from its perch. Luckily, it had only fallen onto its side, only inches from plunging over the cliff into the sea. There had been a local outcry and the lieutenant had been forced to put it back. There were prints in the Logan Rock Inn at Treen, nearby, showing the massive equipment and effort that had finally succeeded in replacing the rock. The itemised bill of costs could also be seen there, and Ben chuckled as he recalled one of the items.

"It even includes the hire of sixty St Just men who did nothing but drink beer to the value of thirteen shillings an' sixpence!"

BUT that had been yesterday. Blue summer skies had given way overnight to the sudden storm. Already, as they battled their way down the old lane, they could see that the Atlantic had become a grey, heaving monster, flecked with white, and could hear the thunderous crash of waves against granite.

Penny stopped abruptly so that her brother cannoned into her. "Look!" She pointed ahead. "What are those flashing blue lights?"

"Ambulances," said Ben. "Police, too, I think. What's going on?"

2: THE WRECK OF THE
MARCEL BRIEUX

THE Breton trawler *Marcel Brieux*, registered in St Malo, had been fishing in the Western Approaches when warning of the storm reached her. She turned and fled, seeking the shelter of Newlyn harbour, but the speed of the storm caught her completely by surprise. With her rudder smashed by the waves, she was driven helplessly towards the coast.

At eight o'clock that morning, coastguards at Tol-pedn heard her Mayday plea over the ship-to-shore radio, and spotted her distress flares a mile or so off the coast. At first, it looked as though the storm would carry her clear of the cliffs and into the calmer waters of Mount's Bay, but the sea had different plans.

At 8.25 she struck, the sea flinging her bodily against the pinnacled headland of Treryn Dinas.

For John and Penny, the sight was terrifying and its horror was reflected by their faces. Two hundred feet below them, the stricken vessel lay on her starboard side beneath overhanging crags, unprotected and at the mercy of a mountainous sea. Wave after huge wave rolled in, each pounding the trawler with murderous intent, then pouring away in readiness for the next. Dense clouds of spray, whipped up by the gale, became a whirling mist through which wailed the mournful lament of the Runnel Stone buoy.

Dimly visible behind the smashed windows of the vessel's wheel-house were white, scared faces of men who knew that their lives depended on the rescuers on the cliff top and in the great naval helicopter which hovered overhead. Further out to sea, the orange and dark blue shapes of the Sennen Cove and Penlee lifeboats vanished briefly into cavernous troughs and reared high on the crests of the following waves.

Time was running out. Each colossal breaker threw the trawler further towards the waiting cliff as though it were no more than a toy which, when the sea had tired of it, would be flung aside and discarded, smashed and twisted beyond all recognition.

The children listened as a coastguard spoke to Ben. "They're in trouble. The chopper can't get to them because of the overhang, and it's too shallow and rough in here for the lifeboats. God knows, we don't want another *Jeanne Gougy*."

Few people on that coast would ever forget the *Jeanne Gougy*. Another Breton trawler, she had struck the cliffs at the Land's End in the November of 1962. The extraordinary skill of the rescuers had saved five of the crew, but eleven men, including the vessel's captain, had died.

A muffled boom only just topped the roar of wind and sea. The aim was true and the line attached to the rocket fell across the wheel-house. There was a brief glimpse of a hand reaching out to grab it before the next wave swept its green and white sheet over the wreck.

Ben looked quizzically at the coastguard. "Breeches-buoy? I thought they'd been withdrawn from service."

The coastguard smiled grimly. "Officially, yes. Some of us reckoned we had more sense than the damn fool who insisted on abolishing them. I think this proves our point. There's no other way of getting those guys off."

The breeches-buoy was assembled with amazing speed and the first of the trawler's crew was soon on his way to the cliff top and safety. Ben and the children listened as the coastguard questioned the fisherman.

"Combien des hommes sur le . . . Oh, for crying out loud, how

many men?" His arms windmilled as he tried to make himself understood. The Breton listened, drenched and shivering from cold and shock, and finally grasped the question.

"*Quatorze* . . . er, fourteen, *oui? Et moi*, fifteen." A blanket was flung around his shoulders and he was hustled off to where the ambulances waited.

Below them, the drama unfolded. One by one the crew of the *Marcel Brieux* clambered through the paneless windows of the wheel-house, strapped themselves into the breeches-buoy, and were hauled the two hundred feet to safety. True to tradition, the skipper was the last to leave his ship. Like his shipmates before him, he climbed out through the wheel-house window, clutching the line and anything else that came to hand, and strapped himself into the harness. A massive wave broke over the ship and, for a moment, he was lost from view. Then, to everyone's relief, he reappeared, still secure in the breeches-buoy, waved cheerfully and began the slow journey to the cliff top.

Some say that every seventh wave is bigger than all the rest. If so, the wave rolling menacingly closer was the grandfather of all seventh waves. The lifeboat crew had already seen it as it built up and were heading out to meet it in deeper water.

The waters of Porthcurno are shallow and as the wave entered the bay so it towered to twice its former height; an immense green wall that dwarfed the stricken ship. The captain, though, was now halfway to the cliff top and appeared to be safe.

The giant wave broke with a tremendous crash, flinging the ship in towards the base of the cliff. The line slackened and throats tightened as the helpless figure dropped thirty feet, only to be brought up with a jerk. The men on the cliff top redoubled their efforts, hauling away for all they were worth.

The wave swept on over the trawler. It smashed into the resilient cliff with a deafening thump, a huge explosion of snowy whiteness that shook the very ground, then rebounded outwards, dragging the wreck with it.

No rope on earth could have withstood it. To the horror of the helpless onlookers, the line snapped, catapulting the captain away in a downward arc to certain death; a sheer drop of eighty feet into the boiling hell below.

John hoped that it was really just a nightmare; that he'd wake up to find the sun streaming through his window. Penny turned away in tears. If the fall hadn't killed the trawlerman, the pounding seas and waiting rocks soon would.

John glanced up and shouted "The helicopter's coming in!" The great Sea King moved slowly in towards the cliff. The gale strove to fling the craft against the rock-face but the pilot's skill was astonishing; calmly compensating for each gust. Even so, there were heart-stopping moments when the whirling rotors were bare inches from smashing themselves to shards on the rock.

An orange-clad figure began to descend on a fragile line, lowered carefully from within the craft. The wind seemed to sense his intrusion, gusting even harder until he was swinging like a pendulum. A sudden surging blast hurled him like a rag doll at the overhanging face of the cliff, but the airman was equal to it, twisting in his harness and using his feet to fend himself away from the rock.

He looked up at his crewmates, signalling frantically, and everyone's heart sank. "He's too close under the cliff," said Ben. "They can't get to him."

The winchman was hauled back into the Sea King which rose away from the cliff to hover uncertainly nearby. Not even the skill of the naval pilot and the courage of the winchman was enough. The body of the Breton, dead or unconscious, was the property of the ocean. The orange splash of his life- jacket which, at least, held him the right way up should he still be alive, was a pathetic spot in the cauldron of the sea. As if in cruel laughter, patches of blue sky began to show far away to the south-west. The storm was abating.

There was one slim chance: an old rescue technique steeped in tradition but fraught with danger. "Come on!" came a shout. "Follow me down. Form a human chain." It was Ben Trevelyan, waving his arms and running towards the edge of the cliff. He had remembered a way down close by. It was precipitous and risky but a way down nonetheless. He spotted a half-forgotten landmark and started forward. John began to run after him. "Go back, John!" roared the farmer. "Stay put. It's too risky." He vanished over the cliff with a dozen men close on his heels.

8

At the bottom, the men formed their human chain, each grasping the wrist of the next. Ben, the tallest of them, tore off his boots and put himself at the head. The chain began to battle its way out through the massive breakers. Time and again they engulfed the farmer but sheer determination carried him through, even though his footing was far from secure on the boulders which rolled beneath his feet. The mammoth effort was in vain; the human chain was hopelessly short.

Having come this far, Ben was in no mood for giving up. The second man in the chain pulled at his wrist to make him stop and turn back but the farmer angrily shook him off. He launched himself into the boiling waves, ignoring the shouts of protest.

The sea fought against him, his clothing weighed him down, but somehow, as the others held their breath, his powerful, desperate strokes brought him within reach of the trawlerman. Ben could not tell if he was alive or dead, but the white face seemed ominously still. He grasped the collar of the life-jacket, twisting it into his grip, and began the haul back to shore. His woollen jersey and corduroy trousers were lead weights, pulling him down. He went under and came up spluttering. What little strength he had left was fast deserting him, his legs ached in every muscle and his head was spinning.

Slowly he slipped beneath the waves. He gasped for breath and breathed in water. Green spirals spun before his eyes, bright lights exploded in his head and he felt a dark cloud beginning to sweep over him.

A rough hand grasped him, hauling him up. His foot struck a boulder on the bottom and he fell, floundering. More hands joined the first and he found himself being dragged ashore. Somehow he had kept a tight grip on the Breton, although his hands were numb. His fingers had to be prised apart to release his hold.

"Easy now, Ben," said a breathless voice. "You're all right; we've got you." Arms guided him from the water, half-leading, half-carrying him to a large boulder where they sat him down, forcing his head down between his knees. He coughed painfully, spitting sea-water, but found his senses clearing. "Is he dead?" he wheezed.

"He's alive, Ben, and tes down to you," said a young, fair-haired fisherman. "The doctor reckons he's got half the bay in him, and a couple o' busted ribs, but he says he'll pull through. Tell 'ee this, pard, I never saw a braver thing . . . or a dafter one."

Ben coughed again, bringing his hand to his mouth. As he did so, he saw that he was holding something he had not noticed before. "What's this?" he said. It was what seemed to be a circular band of metal, heavily encrusted as though it had lain beneath the sea for centuries.

"Habm a clue," said Ben. "P'raps I'll take'n home an' find out."

THE news of the rescue was the talk of St Buryan when Ben and the children called in at the shop the next day. The vicar, a tall, grey-haired man, stopped him outside the shop, and Ben listened patiently to his seemingly endless praise.

At the first opportunity, Ben changed the subject by introducing John and Penny, who shook hands with the vicar. "There's quite a resemblance between John and yourself, Ben," he remarked. "He'll end up with your build, too, I should think."

"P'raps he will," smiled the farmer. "Young Penny's more like her father; my brother Frank, you'll remember him. Where I was always big an' dark, he was quite fair and slighter built – "

He broke off as the ring of a horse's hoofs on tarmac met his ear. "I wonder if this is our friend Mr Milliton?"

The vicar lowered his voice. "If it is, I'll be on my way. You'll forgive me, and it's hardly a Christian thought, but the less contact I have with that gentleman, the easier I feel."

"I don't reckon there's many hereabouts who'll argue with 'ee, Vicar, Christian or no," Ben agreed. The vicar smiled at John and Penny and strode off in the direction of the church.

The cause of their unease was a bearded man riding a coal-black and breathtakingly beautiful mare, whose fine, dished head spoke strongly of Arab blood. Her only marking was a white, diamond-shaped star on her forehead. The rider himself was a curious sight. His clothing was obviously expensive but he wore it carelessly, giving him an unkempt look. His long, dark hair was tousled and untidy and the unmistakeable air of the eccentric hung about him. It was difficult to judge his age; it could have been anywhere from thirty-five to fifty.

He wore a black, old-fashioned jacket over a crumpled, open-necked silk shirt, and black riding breeches were tucked untidily into the tops of his tall leather boots. A pendant of silvery metal swung from his neck, a curious design which appeared to be a star within a circle.

"Good-day to you, Vicar," he called out as he passed close by. The vicar's reply was courteous but subdued.

All at once the tranquillity of the village was shattered. The mare's ears flattened to her skull and, without further warning, her head swung round, eyes rolling, teeth bared and flashing in the sun as she lunged.

The vicar flung up a hand, cried out in pain and fright, and crashed backwards into a garden hedge. Ben reacted quickly, dashing up the road and glaring angrily at the horseman.

"Dammit, Milliton!" he bawled. "Why the hell can't 'ee keep that beast under control?"

Looking mildly shocked, Milliton ignored him and turned his attention to the stricken priest. "My dear Vicar," he said smoothly. "My sincere apologies. I never dreamed she would ever do such a thing. Your jacket – it's torn." He reached inside his jacket. "Please, take this. It will atone for the damage."

The leather pouch hit the road with a dull chink. Ben took little notice. "Come off it, Milliton," he said furiously. "You knaw as well as I do what sort o' temper that animal's got. Now get her home 'fore she has a go at someone else."

Milliton nodded wordlessly and turned the horse away. His expression was one of remorse, shamed and tight-lipped – until he drew near to the corner. By then, his face was hidden from Ben and the vicar, but in full view of John and Penny, who were astonished to see the look change to one of unholy glee. The eccentric's shoulders shook with silent laughter as he patted the mare's neck. Then he turned the corner and was gone.

Ben helped the vicar to his feet. The poor man was ashen-faced and trembling as his frightened eyes sought the farmer's.

"Now get her home!"

"Her eyes, Ben," he whispered. "Did you see? When she went for me – they glowed, Ben. They burned like the very fires of Hell!"

"Just take it quiet, now, Vicar," said Ben, soothingly. "'Tes a nasty fright she's given 'ee. Your jacket's ruined and it looks like she drew blood, too. I'd best get 'ee over to the doctor's."

The vicar drew a deep breath, trying hard to compose himself. "It's good of you, Ben, but I really think it looks worse than it is." He paused, noticing the leather pouch at his feet. He bent to pick it up and loosened the drawstring. His eyes widened as the glittering contents slid out onto his palm.

"Good heavens!" he breathed.

3: THE CROWNSTONE

"I COULDN'T believe my eyes," said Ben that evening. "Those coins must be worth a king's ransom. They were antiques, all of 'em. Sovereigns, groats, even doubloons. Every one in mint condition an' none of 'em less than five hundred years old. Tes funny, I always had the notion that Milliton had a bob or two."

"Who is he?" Penny asked.

"Henry Milliton? Well, that's the strange thing. Apart from his name no one d'knaw for sure. He moved into the area 'bout three or four months back an' bought a ramshackle old cottage out on the Lamorna road. Mostly he keeps hisself to hisself, but there's been the odd funny incident. He's got high an' mighty manners, but he edn a man to be liked or trusted. You said yourself he was laughin' after that foul-tempered 'oss of his bit the vicar."

"You've had quite a time of it," said Nellie Hosken, who had been busy darning a pair of Ben's socks. "All three of 'ee, 'an you 'specially, Ben."

"Iss," said Ned. "But they never gave 'ee a mention on the news."

"Thank God for that," said Ben. "I threatened 'em all within an inch o' their lives if they dropped my name to the Press."

John looked up from the book he'd picked out of Ben's bookshelf. "What was that thing you dragged out of the sea?"

"I'd forgotten about that. Tes still in the Land Rover. Let's find out, if I can find somethin' to chip off all that growth. I'll go an' get'n, an' we can do it on the kitchen table."

He fetched the strange object and found an old geological hammer in a drawer. Everyone gathered round as he chipped delicately away at the hard marine crust which coated the band.

"Tes metal sure 'nough." Ben indicated the small gap he had made in the crust, where a metallic glint showed through. He carried on, painstakingly clearing inch by inch until, at last, the whole object lay revealed.

It was a thin circlet of reddish-yellow metal, about two inches deep and big enough to fit a man's head. At one point, it widened into a diamond shape and set into the centre of this was a single large jewel, multi-faceted and as green as the ocean depths from which it had come.

Penny pointed at the area around the gemstone. "There's some writing on it."

Ben peered closely, gingerly lifting the object and turning it to the light. "You're right, there is, but tedn easy to make out. It starts with A ... N ... Then there's a gap. John, write this down, can 'ee? There's some paper in the bureau. Oh, there should be a magnifying glass there, too." He waited for John to return. "C ... V ... that edn right, surely? I think the next letter's an R, then another V and either an H or an N."

John frowned. "Doesn't make sense."

Ben carried on, reading out the letters one by one, then took the sheet of paper. "Still makes no sense." John shrugged. On the paper he had written four words:

AN CVRVN ARLYDHY LYONES

The blood drained from Ben's face. "It does make sense, you! Tedn English or Latin. Tes old Cornish! See, the V's are U's." He got up, vanished into the living-room and came back with a thick book. "This'll do the job: English Cornish dictionary," he explained, flicking through its pages.

"Ah, here tes. CURUN means crown."

He gasped, sitting bolt upright. "I've got it! Oh, my dear lord, what have we found? I can't believe it . . . This is going to change history!"

Penny squirmed with impatience. "Come on, Ben, tell us what it says!"

"Not for a minute. Look, there's more writing here, much smaller. It goes most of the way round." He peered through the magnifying glass. "Names. Dozens of 'em. AN ARLETH RIVALYN . . . AN ARLETH TRISTAN . . . I wonder if that was the Tristan of the King Arthur stories?"

"Wasn't Sir Tristan's father called Rivalyn?" said John, but Ben wasn't listening.

"Look! Look at this! The last name of all! See it, can 'ee? AN ARLETH TREVYLYAN! The lord Trevelyan!"

They looked confusedly at him. "Don't 'ee understand? Course, you wouldn't know, would 'ee? Come with me." He led them back into the living-room and pointed at a coat of arms mounted high on the stone chimney breast. Within its shield were alternate blue and white wavy lines and, emerging from them, a white horse. Beneath the device was the motto: TYME TRYETH TROTH.

"The Trevelyan coat of arms," explained Ben. "The white horse is supposed to have carried our ancestor from the flood which swallowed up the Lyonesse, which was an ancient land that legend says used to exist between the Land's End an' the Isles o' Scilly. The story goes back some fifteen 'undred year to when King Arthur fought his last battle against the traitor Sir Medraut. After the battle, when King Arthur lay dead, Medraut's army chased what was left of Arthur's men down through Cornwall to the Lyonesse, intent on killing 'em all. There the ghost of Merlin appeared, an' cast a terrible spell. The sea rose up an' swallowed the land of Lyonesse forever, drowning Medraut an' all his men. The King's men were saved, because they'd reached the tops of the hills which are now the Isles o' Scilly."

He paused for a moment. "Now, as the tidal wave rushed in, a man on a white horse was seen to gallop from the capital city of the Lyonesse, which was where the Seven Stones are, towards the mainland. He only just made it, for the wave picked 'im up an' dumped 'im on the hill-side under the Sennen, close to the Land's End.

"This man was a native of the Lyonesse, an' was its only survivor. His name was Trevelyan, ancestor of the Trevelyan family. Now, that crown in there has the words: THE CROWN OF THE LORDS OF LYONESSE. It's got the names o' Rivalyn an' Tristan . . . they were said to have come from there. An' then the last name . . . The Lord Trevelyan. Now d'you understand? Course," he shrugged, "the experts do reckon tes all a load o' nonsense. What we've got here is the proof!"

"It's strange that it should be found by a Trevelyan," Penny remarked. "But it's fantastic. Our ancestor . . . lord of a land that doesn't exist any more."

"We've got some hard-headed thinking to do," said Ben. "I doubt we'll be able to keep it. Tes too old an' valuable. It'll probably have to go to a museum; maybe the County one in Truro. The British Museum may want 'en, but I'll put my foot down if they do. It shouldn't be allowed to leave Cornwall, it b'longs here, not up there in London. I'll give Truro a ring in the mornin'. They'll want to date'n but, if the legend is right, it'll date from the sixth century."

"It'll be older than that, won't it?" John interrupted. "I mean, there's a lot of names on it, and if the Lyonesse was drowned in the sixth century – ?"

"Damme, the boy's right!" Ben exclaimed. "There's close on fifty names there an' if the lords ruled for, what, say twenty years on average?" He paused to work it out and whistled. "Then 'twould date from around 500 BC!"

Nellie got up. As excited as everyone else, she tried to find words to match the discovery, but all that came out was: "I'll go an' make us all a cup o' tay." She vanished into the kitchen, half in a dream.

"You realise, don't 'ee," said Ben, "that there's no price anyone can put – "

From the kitchen came a sudden, startled cry and the smash of crockery. They all leapt to their feet, rushing to see what had happened. The shattered remains of a saucer lay on the quarry-tiled floor, but Nellie wasn't looking at that. She stared, thunderstruck, at the kitchen table, where the crown had been.

The Crown of the Lords of Lyonesse had gone, crumbled away, leaving a ring of ochre dust from which the green jewel, all that was left intact, winked innocently up at them.

"I WONDER what made it do that?" mused John, staring into the muddy depths of his coffee.

"Do what?" Penny turned away from the view. The café window looked out over Penzance harbour and across the sandy bay to the breath-taking cone of St Michael's Mount.

"Why did it crumble away like that?"

"I don't know. Maybe when all that crust came off, being exposed to the air was too much for it. It'd been under the sea for centuries."

John pursed his lips, unconvinced. "But what metal would do that? I mean, it wasn't iron. There wasn't any rust. Ben said it wasn't Cornish tin, either. Tin looks silvery."

"Still trying to puzzle it out?" said Ben, joining them.

"You've been gone ages," said Penny, accusingly.

The farmer gravely consulted his watch. "I'm only ten minutes late."

"And I can smell beer," she carried on.

"You're a right little nagger," Ben grinned. "'Twas only the one. I like to drop into the Dolphin when I come into Penzance. Anyhow, I've been doin' other things as well." He dipped into a voluminous pocket and brought out a little book.

"For you, John. Tes a handy little guide to the area. New out and much better than any o' the others you can get. That'll tell 'ee much more 'bout West Cornwall than I can, an' it's got some good little maps, too. Now, for you, Penny, somethin' a little special to wear round your neck."

She gasped as he produced the pendant. There in his hand glittered the gemstone from the crown, now in a new setting attached to a slender chain.

"Old friend o' mine did that," Ben explained. "He's a jeweller. Funny thing, though, the stone had him stumped. He didn't have a clue what it was. Tedn no emerald, he's sure o' that, or any other kind o' precious stone he's ever seen. On the other hand, he says tes no fake either. I figured that, with the crown gone, so has our proof that the Lyonesse ever existed. The stone on its own edn proof of anythin' so I thought we'd keep it in the family an' let the truth be our secret."

Penny put it on, fascinated by the way it caught the light. "It's beautiful. I'll never, ever, take it off. I don't know what to say, Ben."

"Then don't even try," he chuckled. "The look on your face says it all for me. Come on, let's head for home. The scenic route this time."

Ben's scenic route involved driving along Penzance's long promenade to the fishing port of Newlyn. He had gone this way after collecting them from the railway station, but on that occasion had turned right, along Newlyn Combe, to the Land's End road. This time he turned left along the harbour with its fleet of trawlers, some from as far away as Grimsby and Aberdeen. The road led south from Newlyn, hugging the coast all the way and passing the great dusty gash of the Penlee quarry, to enter the former fishing village of Mousehole. "Tedn Mousehole," said Ben, "tes Mowzel."

The streets of the village were narrow and twisted all over the place, but they were soon through and climbing the steep Raginnis Hill, from which they could look back over the village and its tiny, ancient harbour huddling behind the protection of the flat, rocky St Clement's Isle. The view extended to include Penzance and the whole of Mount's Bay – perhaps one of the most beautiful bays in Europe.

Ben then drove inland, joining the road which led down into the Lamorna valley with its woods and an old mill which still kept its great wheel. He slowed near the top of the opposite slope to point out a pair of huge standing stones in fields to the right of the road. The taller stood close to a farm. Slightly leaning, it jutted aggressively to a height of some fifteen feet. The other, only a foot or so shorter, stood about a hundred yards away.

"They're somethin' like four thousand years old," Ben told them, "an' they're called the Pipers of Boleigh. There's an old

tale which says that the Pipers were turned to stone for whoopin'
it up on a Sunday. They were playin' music for the Merry
Maidens to dance to. We'll see them in a minute."

After turning a couple of tight bends, and passing an old stone
Celtic cross by the roadside, Ben stopped the Land Rover. He
climbed out and John and Penny followed him to a granite stile
where they met a sight which had come down through the annals
of time.

Nineteen upright stones stood in a wide but perfect circle in
the centre of a grassy field. "The Merry Maidens," Ben announced. "Cornish folk used to call 'en Dawns Mein, which
means the Stone Dance. Tes really a Bronze Age circle, but if the
old tale takes your fancy, you'll see another menhir – standing
stone – in a field hedge across the road. He was the Fiddler, who
finished up the same way as the Pipers an' the Maidens. An' so
will I," he added, "if I forget to pick up some bread for Nellie. I
meant to do that in Penzance, so we'd best head for the shop in
St Buryan."

THEY stopped in the centre of the village, opposite the church.
Ben and John went into the shop while Penny wandered over to
admire the age-old stone cross near the churchyard wall.

The calm, unhurried sound of a horse's hoofs came round the
corner. Penny swung round. It was Henry Milliton, as usual
riding his mare. He brought the horse to a halt beside Penny

"Remarkable monument, don't you think?" he remarked
pleasantly..

"Yes, it is," Penny agreed. She looked at the horse which
stood obedient to her master's touch. "She really is beautiful. Is
she an Arab?"

Milliton smiled proudly. "Pure-blooded, but of unusual
breeding. I would go as far as to say that she is unique."

"What's her name?"

"Leila," said Milliton. "An Arab name, fittingly enough. It
means 'She of the Night.'"

"It suits her," said Penny, reaching out to stroke the elegantly
arched neck. The mare stiffened, laying her ears back, showing
the whites of her eyes and slanting her nostrils in hostility. The

girl drew her hand away and Milliton leant forward to mutter unintelligibly into the horse's ear. The mare relaxed immediately.

"There," said Milliton. "Now you can stroke her."

Hesitantly, Penny raised her hand and softly ran her fingers down the glossy neck. The mare rubbed her muzzle gently against her shoulder as if to show that no offence had really been meant.

"You see?" smiled Milliton. "Just a one-man horse, really. She's not so bad." His smile revealed perfect teeth and Penny found herself thinking that if only he took the trouble to tidy himself up, he'd be quite good-looking.

"Does the vicar know that?" She grinned cheekily.

Milliton chuckled. "I don't imagine he would," he said. "To be serious, though, that little episode was most regrettable. I'm afraid that Leila has her likes and dislikes. For reasons known only to her, the vicar seems to fall into the second category, though I never thought she'd go that far.

"It doesn't help that I don't rate very highly in the vicar's esteem. Perhaps he knows that I am not a Christian. I fell out of love with the Christian church a great many years ago." He gestured down at her, changing the subject. "That's a pretty pendant. In this light, the stone looks genuine. Most unusual. It suits you."

"I think it might be very old . . ." Penny caught his eye and found she could not look away. The dark eyes held her gaze and a sudden wave of giddiness swept over her. She tottered. The church tower and surrounding cottages seemed to spin around her in dizzying circles. She gasped for breath, the blood drained from her face and roared in her ears.

"Mr Milliton!" The urgent voice cut through the whirling vortex. Penny staggered, then, all at once, her head was clear. She blinked, and there was the vicar hurrying across the road, waving the leather money pouch. Milliton ignored him and leant towards Penny, his brows knotted with concern.

"Are you all right? You went quite pale for a moment."

"I think so. I felt faint all of a sudden. P'raps I've caught a touch of the sun."

"Mr Milliton!" It was the vicar again, standing well out of

reach of the black horse, which regarded him with ill-concealed hostility. "I really must talk to you about these coins."

A flash of irritation crossed Milliton's face as he turned to the priest. "What of them?" he said coldly. "They were to compensate for the damage done by the mare. The incident was regrettable and should not have happened."

"But their value, man! Have you any idea? They are valuable antiques and, without exception, in mint condition. They are worth a fortune!"

Milliton cut him short. "Their value means nothing to me. There are many more where they came from. It is no loss."

"But I cannot accept them," the vicar persisted. "The only damage was to a jacket and a shirt, and a very small cut on my arm. These coins could purchase half the village. I'm sorry, Mr Milliton, you must take them back."

"I will not," said Milliton shortly. "Do what you will with them. I am sure a man of the cloth such as you will find a worthy cause to put them to."

"But . . ."

"Please, Vicar; the matter is closed." Milliton turned back to Penny, leaving the vicar standing in the road with his mouth opening and closing soundlessly, like a landed fish. "Young lady, your friends are waiting for you," he said. "I enjoyed our conversation, but you're still looking a little pale. If I were you, my dear, I'd go home and lie down for a while."

"WHAT did he want?" said Ben, staring at Milliton's back as he trotted sedately away.

"Nothing really," Penny replied. "Just chatting. He was admirin away.

"Nothing really," Penny replied. "Just chatting. He was admiring my pendant."

"Was he now? Quite honestly, I'd be a lot happier if 'ee kept well clear of friend Milliton. Don't let his manners fool 'ee. There's somethin' very wrong 'bout him, not to mention that foul-tempered 'oss of his. If mine were like that, I'd get well shot of 'em."

"I didn't know you had horses," said Penny.

"I don't s'pose you'll have seen 'em. They're down the bottom field; four of 'em. There's my big hunter, a brood mare an' a couple o' fourteen-'anders. The ponies belonged to my wife; adored 'em, she did. So, after she died . . . well, I couldn't bear to part with 'em. She raised 'em, broke 'em in an' schooled 'em on . . . They were part of her, if you see what I mean." His eyes looked lost and far away for a moment.

"Anyhow," he went on, "do you two ride?"

"Yes, both of us," said John. "Penny's better than me, but then she rides more often."

"Couldn't be better. We'll 'ave the ponies up this afternoon, an' see how you two shape up. You shouldn't 'ave any trouble; good as gold, they are. Normally, a couple o' kids from the village ride 'em an' take in gymkhanas an' that, so they're pretty fit. I always reckon the best way to explore this district is on horseback, 'specially up on the moors."

4: THE POWER AND THE CIRCLE

"ARE there any more stone circles near here?" asked Penny over breakfast.

"There's a beauty a mile or so north o' the village," said Ben, reaching for the marmalade jar. "Tes called Boscawen-ûn." He pronounced the curious name 'Bscow-noon'. "Tes a bit different from the Merry Maidens 'cause there's a tall stone right in the middle of 'en. Tes worth going to see. They've held the Cornish Gorseth there a couple o' times."

"Cornish what?" said John.

"Gorseth. A gathering o' bards. People who've done a lot for Cornwall in some way are made bards. You see, in spite o' what some people d'think, Cornwall edn no more a part of England than Wales or Scotland are. Tes a Celtic land an' we're Celtic people, who've been in Britain thousands o' years longer than the English. We even had our own kings once, an' lots o' the old traditions are still carried on. We've even got our own language, as I've told 'ee. It near died out a century or so back, but tes growing again. Quite a few people can speak 'en.

"The Gorseth is a sight to see. All the bards in long blue

robes, p'raps a couple o' hundred of 'en, all in a big circle. There's harp music, an' a huge sword which represents King Arthur's sword. The whole thing's conducted in the language: *Nyns-yu marow Myghtern Arthur*," he finished, grandly.

Penny blinked at him. "Was that Cornish?"

Ben nodded. "'King Arthur is not dead.' That's the old Celtic belief."

"He'll be ancient if he isn't," John remarked.

The farmer laughed. "A good fifteen 'undred years old. Historians reckon that the real Arthur lived at the beginning of the sixth century. Some even think he wadn' really a king at all; more a roving cavalry general who wound up as commander of the British resistance against the Saxon invasion. No knights in shining armour goin' round rescuin' damsels, not even a Round Table or a Grail. They came into the story much later. He probably spent most of his time covered in mud an' travel dust, an' stinkin' o' sweat an' horses."

"I'd rather stick to the Round Table and gallant knights," sniffed Penny.

"I wouldn't," John chipped in. "I think a scruffy warlord galloping all over the country and winning battles sounds much better. I mean, he's made out to be such a goody-goody in the books. Boring. I'll bet he was really bloodthirsty."

"I'd rather have the King Arthur of the books," said Penny, huffly.

"I think we ought to change the subject 'fore we 'ave a war right here," Ben said quickly. "Now, this stone circle. You go up to the village an' take the left turn at the church . . . there's probably a map in that book I gave 'ee, John. It'll go in your pocket. Why don't 'ee take the ponies, so long as you mind the traffic."

JOHN's map-reading left something to be desired, and it was early afternoon before they finally came across the stone circle of Boscawen-ûn. It was a strange, timeless sight. On the side of a lonely valley stood a wide ring of nineteen grey stones, surrounded by bramble and bracken which half-hid the circular stone hedge encircling the monument. Each stone was about four feet high and near the centre of the circle stood another, twice the height of the others and leaning sharply.

They tethered the ponies and walked through a gap in the hedge to enter the circle. Penny stood in silence for a while, gazing in wonder at the ancient stones around her.

"There's a sort of. . . a feeling about this place." Her voice was hushed, as though she were speaking inside a church. "Have you noticed?"

John kept his thoughts to himself, not wanting to admit to any such thing. Nonetheless, he had sensed the peculiar silence and sanctity of the place. It was unnaturally quiet. The horizon shimmered under the sun and the only sound was the brief, contented low of a cow in a nearby field. He puzzled over the fact that, where the air should have been filled with the hum of a thousand insects, there was no sound at all.

"I wonder how old it is?" said Penny.

"The book reckons it could be four thousand years old."

"As old as that? I wonder what it was used for."

"Didn't Ben say something about prehistoric religion?"

"Oh, yes." Penny moved to the big central stone. "Maybe the High Priest, or whatever they had, stood here." She laid a hand on the rough surface of the monolith, gazing up at its cap of golden lichen.

Now that was strange. She could have sworn that the great stone had moved beneath her touch. She smiled at her own imagination. The smile vanished. It had moved again; this time she was certain.

"John." Her voice sounded woefully small. "The stone's moving."

He looked round, frowning. "Don't be daft. It'd take more than you and me together to shift that."

"But it is!" she insisted. "I can feel it. It's shaking!"

"Come off it! There's not the slightest . . ." John stopped in midstream, gaping. "Penny! The stone! LOOK AT THE STONE!"

She looked up sharply and sank to her knees in terror.

The cap of the stone was no longer one of golden lichen, but one of light. A slowly pulsing ball of blue-white fire sat on the very tip of the pillar, and it hurt their eyes to look at it.

Penny caught sight of the ancient jewel in her pendant and her eyes widened. It was alive, emitting a bright greenish light which pulsed in time with the globe of light on the ancient monolith.

A humming sound filled their ears. The very air began to throb and thrum like a great engine and the ground beneath their feet swayed, throwing them off balance. Beyond the circle, the ponies whinnied in fright, tugging wildly at their tethers.

There was a sudden, ear-splitting crack, and a bright flash which made them reel away, momentarily blinded. When their vision returned, they saw that each stone of the circle now had its own cap of brilliant blue light. Giant sparks arc'd from stone to stone, and spiralled in towards the central pillar. Their scalps tingled with the electric charge and streaks of light flashed through the ground, shooting outward from the circle in every direction as if it was the hub of a gigantic, living wheel.

The ponies had quietened and now stood facing the ring of stones, heads high and ears pricked. Every hair of their coats shone and lights played in their eyes.

"Get out!" John bawled through the dreadful buzz and crackle. "Get out of the circle!"

"I can't! I can't move!"

"Try! Come on, you have to try!"

It was as if a whirlpool was relentlessly sucking them in towards its centre. It took an immense effort of body and mind to move, but move they did, gritting their teeth and crawling, gasping with the strain, towards the edge of the circle.

Penny looked up at the blue arcs leaping from stone to stone, and her heart quailed. "No! I can't go through that!"

John grabbed her collar and hauled her between the stones. Their hair stood on end and they prickled all over with the electricity. Then they were out: free of the circle and all its terrors. They lay gasping on the grass.

"We made it!" wheezed John. "But why – ?" His words faltered as he stared back at the circle in disbelief.

Before them stood a ring of nineteen grey stones, with a tall, leaning pillar, capped with golden lichen, near the centre; silent and unmoving, timeless and mysterious.

Each stone now had its own cap of brilliant light

"I don't understand," said Penny in a small, lost voice. "I don't understand."

"NO more do I," spoke a gruff voice that held a trace of anger. "Why must men always meddle with matters which do not concern them?"

Startled, John and Penny jumped up, gaping stupidly as the newcomer approached. Never had they seen anyone so strange. Stockily built, he was hardly taller than the stones of the circle. His clothing was of supple brown leather; tunic, breeches and high boots. A cloak, the colour of leaves in autumn, swung from the wide shoulders, and a vicious, double-bladed axe rested behind his belt. A horned helmet of bronze sat firmly on his head and a grave, wind-blown face was framed by dark hair and a full, heavy beard. Dark eyes glittered as he stalked towards them.

"Who are you?" said Penny, hesitantly.

"Is it not I who should be asking that of you?" came the growled reply. The dwarf paused as he caught sight of the jewel, gleaming innocently at the end of its long chain. He reached out a hand and took a step towards Penny.

"You leave her alone!" said John. He stepped forward threateningly, then froze in his tracks.

The dwarf had moved to meet the threat with uncanny speed, whirling and dropping to a crouch, poised and prepared. The axe had somehow conjured itself into his hand, raised and ready for the strike.

"Come to your senses, boy!" he rasped. "Learn who it is you threaten. Gawen am I, son of Gwalchmai, and greater heads than yours have fallen to the axe of Gawen the dwarf. Now," he said, standing up and relaxing, "cool that hot head of yours. I intend no harm to either one of you."

He twirled the axe by the leather thong attached to its handle, and slid it back behind his belt. Turning back to Penny, he gently took the pendant and studied it thoughtfully.

"How did you come by this?" he said, releasing it. Penny looked at her brother for guidance, but he shrugged his shoulders and said nothing. The dwarf listened intently as she told him of the shipwreck and the finding of the crown.

"So," he said quietly. "The Crownstone of Lyonesse. After all this time, it comes back from the sea. It explains many things, not least what I have seen here." He waved a hand at the stone circle. "Within that pretty bauble lies a hefty power placed there long ago by the greatest magicians of the Lyonesse. Many were its uses, most now forgotten, but among them was the protection of the Lords of Lyonesse.

"Another ancient power, older, greater and beyond all mortal wizardry, was locked within this circle. The Crownstone has released it, whether for good or ill I cannot tell. Probably both. We call it the Breath of the Dragon and it is a secret of the Earth Mother herself. Good and ill have no meaning for it; it does not distinguish the one from the other."

"What rubbish!" John snorted. "Why are you trying to frighten us with all that clap-trap?"

The dwarf stared at him for a moment, then pointed meaningfully at the circle. "Seeing is believing, boy. The men of this world have strayed far indeed from the old knowledge! They deny and scorn that which lies before their very eyes, and still they cannot see. Well, boy, we do see, and we remember. Because of this, when men are no more, we shall remain."

John looked awkwardly at him.

"Now," said Gawen, "as I have made myself known to you, who might you be?"

His eyes widened as they told him their names. "Trevelyan!" he cried. "Oh, why did you not tell me sooner? There is the sense of it: as the Lord Trevelyan was the last to wear it, so it has sought and found his descendants. Now that the Crownstone is found, something of what I have lately seen and heard also makes some sense . . . and there are things which disturb me. After centuries, the Witch-Lord walks this land again and I do not have to look far to guess why. I warn you now: be wary of this man. He is perilous beyond your understanding."

"Now look!" John burst out angrily, "just what do you mean by that? What is all this about a . . . what was it? Witch-Lord?"

"Do not mock a second time," said the dwarf, this time without anger. "I warn you with all seriousness, but even I lack full knowledge. I must speak with one who is wiser in these matters than I. Only then will any of us know what we face.

"My advice to you is to return to your home and not stray beyond its walls until morning. Say nothing of this to anyone and remember my words: do not roam abroad after dark. At dawn tomorrow, meet with me at the headland of Treryn Dinas, by the Logan Stone."

He turned, climbed the hedge and dropped from sight.

"Hang on a minute!" cried John.

"Remember, dawn tomorrow," came the voice, then the dwarf had gone and so cunningly did he conceal himself as he moved that they caught no further sight of him.

PENNY ate her supper in silence. She appeared to be deep in her own thoughts, and John noticed that her fingers repeatedly strayed to her pendant, but he said nothing.

"What's up with Penny?" Ben whispered into his ear.

"Oh, nothing as far as I know. Just tired, I expect. We rode a bit further than we intended." He grinned sheepishly. "My map-reading's a bit rusty."

Ben chuckled. "I see. Well, apart from gettin' lost, did 'ee enjoy your day?"

"I'll say. We went up on that hill, Chapel Carn something."

"Brea," said Ben, prounouncing it 'bray'. "Chapel Carn Brea."

"Super view from up there. We could see the Scillies. After that we went looking for that stone circle."

"Find it, did 'ee?"

"Eventually." John bit his lip. "Weird sort of place, isn't it?"

AFTER supper, Penny decided to go for a walk around the farm. John thought about going with her, but decided that his company wouldn't be appreciated.

It was pleasant to wander through the fields in the cool evening air. Cows gazed detachedly at her, endlessly, lazily, chewing. The sun was setting, lending everything a reddish tint and, to the north, its dying rays touched the tower of St Buryan church, turning it a coppery hue, but Penny was too preoccupied to notice.

She emerged from her thoughts for a moment to take stock of where she was. Four fields away, the farmhouse chimneys were just visible. In the corner of the field where she stood, hard to distinguish in the gathering gloom, were the overgrown ruins of the original farm, Trehelya Veor. So this was the field called Park Crellas: field of the ruin. Hadn't Ben said something about it being haunted?

She shrugged and turned away, sinking back into her brooding thoughts. The words of the dwarf preyed on her mind, refusing to go away. His words came back to her, over and over: The Witch-Lord walks . . . be wary of this man. What did he mean? Who is this Witch-Lord? The Witch-Lord walks . . . the Witch-Lord.

"Who is the Witch-Lord?" she cried out. The loudness of her own cry startled her, and a flock of crows rattled noisily into the air.

"Witch-Lord" cried the echo. "Witch-Lord . . . Lord . . . Lord."

The echoes died away and the stillness of the evening seemed suddenly oppressive.

"Who is the Witch-Lord?"

The words floated back to her ears and her heart turned to ice, for this time it was no echo. It was a cold whisper; mocking, cruel and wholly evil.

5: NIGHT HUNTERS

PENNY froze. The blood in her veins seemed to shoot down to her feet, rooting her to the spot, and she stood like a statue in the deepening twilight, scarcely daring to breathe.

There was utter silence; a dark, unreal emptiness, until an owl hooted in the depths of the valley below. Penny blinked. The thumping of her heart sounded frighteningly loud.

Had a whispering voice mocked her? Or had the events of the day, the onset of night, the haunted ruin in the corner of the field behind her combined to play cruel tricks on her already confused mind?

She giggled foolishly and turned to go back to the farmhouse. The laughter died in her throat. She wanted to scream; the sound welled up inside her like a balloon, but only a strangled croak emerged.

On the far side of the field, in front of the old, overgrown ruin, stood seven horsemen; a sinister line of motionless shadows. Dark were the horses they sat on, dark their flowing robes and deep the cowls which hid their faces. The central figure stood proud of the rest. He lifted his head and cold points of light glittered from beneath his hood. The horsemen moved forward as one, unhurried and controlled.

Terror became panic. Penny turned and fled. The riders stood between her and the farm, but she neither knew in what direction she was running, nor cared as long as the way led to safety.

She scrambled over gates and stone hedges, but the horsemen still seemed to be in no hurry. Always, when she glanced fearfully around, they were the full width of a field away, cantering slowly. The sound of cruel laughter came to her ears. It was a hunt, callous and deliberate. They were playing her as a cat plays a mouse before the final kill.

Hard tarmac jarred her feet as she jumped down from a high bank. It was the road, twisting steeply down into the darkness of the Penberth valley. She fled down the hill, under the whispering trees at the bottom, and up the far side. The hill soaked up her strength, weariness and fear adding leaden weights to her legs, and her breath came in sobs and gasps. She stopped, but only for a second. The ring of hoofs could be clearly heard on the road at the foot of the valley. She stumbled on, hoping for a turning off the main road. As if in answer to her prayers, a side turning appeared on the left. There were houses, but her senses told her that no ordinary house would provide any sanctuary from these hunters. An inn-sign creaked in the gentle breeze. She glanced up at the sound and caught sight of the picture it carried. It was of a man, pushing at a great rock and toppling it. It stirred a chord of memory and she stared at it, furiously racking her brains. Beneath the picture, the name of the inn seemed suddenly to leap out at her. The Logan Rock.

Hope surged inside her. She was in the village of Treen, and the ancient cliff castle of Treryn Dinas lay nearby. The face of the dwarf Gawen, and his gruff words, floated through her mind: "Meet with me at the headland of Treryn Dinas, by the Logan Stone . . . one who is wiser in these matters than I . . . "

She forced herself to go on through the tiny village and onto the footpath which led down to the cliffs. At the first stile she looked back to see the first of the riders already emerging from between the houses.

Penny leapt down from the hedge and, as she did so, caught sight of an eerie glow at her breast. Just as it had done at the stone circle of Boscawen- ûn, the Crownstone of Lyonesse was shining with a bright, emerald light. This time, it did not pulse, but shone steady and unwavering, then, without warning, a beam flashed from the jewel to the ground, and the narrow path before her lit up; countless thousands of tiny, gossamer strands of light meshing together to show her the way. Her weariness fell from her and her feet seemed to sprout wings. She felt as light as a dandelion seed and ran on, faster and effortlessly.

Behind her, thin, urgent voices raised in angry surprise and the steady beat of the horses' hoofs turned quickly to a frenzied gallop. They spurned the path, spreading out to either side. The riders bent low over the necks of their horses, which leapt the high hedges with uncanny ease. The game was over. Now the hunt was on in earnest, and death rode with the night-hunters.

On she fled until, gasping once more with fear, she scrambled over the final stile. The unearthly light went out. Before her loomed the formidable outer rampart of the prehistoric fort and, to her horror and utter despair, a figure blocked the entrance. It held a lantern and stood motionless, a slim silhouette against the darkening sky.

Penny gave a sob and sank, defeated, to her knees. Hoofs thundered all around her. A leather-clad hand seized her shoulder with a grip of iron, hauling her roughly to her feet. She cried out with the cold, biting pain, and her blood turned to ice.

Above the clamour, a voice rang out. It was clear and commanding and, in spite of the pain, she thrilled to the sound of it. Young and yet ageless, it was the voice of light, of leaves, of summer. A voice of victory.

"Depart this place, demon! The Lord of Castle Treryn denies you your prey. Here is sacred ground where you cannot walk, and the maid has earned sanctuary. Release her. Return to the mists from whence you came!"

The rider's reply was harsh and insolent. "Waste not your words, Lord of the Castle Sacred. I know full well who and what you are: the last of your kind in Belerion. Take care lest Belerion be rid of your kind forever. Even you can find death at the point of a sword. We know where we cannot pass, but we are not yet within the confines of the castle. Your words hold no threat to me; a plague on them! What I have claimed, I will keep!"

It was always difficult for Penny to remember clearly what happened next. As she was being dragged savagely away, a shrill cry of anguish lanced through her head and the icy grip was suddenly released. There was no more pain, just a numbness in her shoulder, as she fell headlong to stare with horrified fascination into fathomless depths.

From the entrance to the cliff castle flowed a river of light, streaming through the very earth itself to where she lay. It was as if she was gazing down into an ocean world of incandescent blue. Rivers of ice flowed into one another, some moving as tranquil streams, others as raging torrents, eddying and bursting into spray of unbearable brightness. There were other forms there, too, but indistinct. The harder she tried to catch sight of them, the more elusive they became, moving deeper into untold, uncharted depths.

The light went out as though someone had flicked a switch, and she found herself staring at dust, stones and blades of stunted grass. Behind her, horses stamped and snorted nervously.

Fearfully, she turned to look. There in the dusk were seven black horses, trembling and foam-flecked, but of their riders there was not a trace.

"It is over," said the stranger, "for tonight." There was a slight intonation in his voice, as though he were unused to speaking English. He moved forward and the lantern swung in his hand.

He was tall, but slightly built. He wore a cloak of sheepskin and his lightly sandalled feet made scarcely a sound as he walked. He carried a deeply curved longbow, and a quiver filled with slim, white-feathered arrows hung from his belt. The lamplight reflected from a tunic of the finest mail and played on his flowing hair, its sheen now silver, now golden. His face was angular, with a straight, finely chiselled nose and high, tilted cheekbones. His mouth was straight, his expression tranquil but with a hint of curiosity.

As he came closer, he held the lantern higher, and its light at last revealed his eyes which had been hidden in shadow.

Penny gasped and shrank back in alarm.

Large and slightly slanted, the dark green eyes were totally, unbelievably, blank. They were expressionless pools of deep emerald, with no trace of either whites or pupils that she could see.

'He's blind!' was her first thought. 'But then . . . why does he need a lantern?' She edged backwards, keeping distance between them. Something warm and unyielding barred her way and she turned to stare into the eyes of one of the horses. The dark orbs stared back at her. Penny caught her breath and turned back to the stranger, whose eyes were so similar.

"You are young," he said gently, "you are human and have seen much that is frightening and beyond your understanding. Be comforted, there is nothing more to fear." Briefly, he took her hands in his, and she felt an instant calm descend on her.

He moved on past her to the horses. "First, I must tend to these unhappy creatures, whose minds can be injured far more easily than your own. These are earthly horses, innocent of all evil, who have suffered much at the hands of the hunters. Their place is in the meadows from which they were taken."

His extraordinary gaze left her to look concernedly at the nervous animals. His voice, as he spoke to them, was soft and soothing, and the words he uttered were of no language that Penny knew. He lightly touched the forehead of each horse in turn and, one by one, they wheeled away, cantering off along the cliff path and into the night. Two remained, free of all fear and nervousness.

Penny could scarcely believe what she had witnessed. "They understood!" she breathed. "They understood every word. It's like . . . magic!"

The slanted brows drew together. "Magic?" he repeated. "I would not have said so. Sorcery is beyond my hand. My people have always spoken with bird and beast, as once did your own. But, as time has passed, so humankind has thought more of itself, and less of the world around it and so it has lost the art."

"But if magic is beyond you," she persisted, "what about that light in the ground. It was you who controlled that, wasn't it?"

He inclined his head. "That is so," he conceded, "but it is older and differs much from magic and the arts of sorcery. The light you saw is a secret of the earth itself, akin to the

Its light at last revealed his eyes

Dragon-breath which was released today at Boscawen-ûn – by yourself, if I am not mistaken. An important difference is that the power here brings agony to the creatures of evil. So it proved with the Nôshelyas, the night-hunters. It has driven them back to the Shadowlands, but it will only be for this one night. It has not the means to destroy them.

"Here, at Castle Treryn, within the rocking stone itself, this earth-power has a storehouse and, as I am lord here, so I am granted the means to contain or release it. That is all."

Penny regarded the strange, impassive figure carefully, and a little fearfully. A voice within her tried to assure her that all was well, that this was a friend, but there were so many questions.

"You talked about 'your people'", she said. "Who are 'your people'? Who are you?"

He stared at her, paused in thought, then shook his head. "It would be unwise for me to answer you until I know more of your part in this matter. Should it prove to be as my heart tells me, then, perhaps you will find the answers you seek. However, I recognise that patience in humankind is not a common virtue."

He motioned her to one of the waiting horses. "This night will harbour no further terrors, but the minds of the young can fear much that is not there. So, I will escort you to the safety of your home, but ask no further questions of me. I fear that the answers would be too much for you to accept."

His strength surprised her as he lifted her effortlessly onto the back of the nearest horse, before springing lightly onto the other.

6: A FORGOTTEN RACE

THE iron-grey light of morning had barely begun to filter into the sky when John slipped quietly into his sister's room. She lay awake, staring dull-eyed at the window.

"Don't you think you ought to tell me what happened last night?" he demanded, keeping his voice low.

"I don't know what you mean!" she protested.

"Sssh! Keep your voice down. Look, you might find it easy to pull the wool over Ben's eyes, but I know you better. You were out for ages, even after dark when you were warned not to be. Then in you come, white as a sheet, and slope off to bed with hardly a word to anyone. That's not exactly normal behaviour for you. Now, put yourself in my shoes and ask yourself what you would've made of that. Now tell me that everything was hunky-dory. So, what happened?"

Penny drew a long breath. "No." she said. "It's no use. You'd never believe a word of it. Come to that, I've been lying here wondering if it really did happen."

John frowned, thinking back to the events of the previous day: the stone circle, the dwarf. "Tell me, anyway," he said. "Think about yesterday at Boscawen-n. I can't deny what happened to us there, can I?"

Reluctantly, she told him of the hunters, the horrible chase and of its strange, wondrous ending. With each sentence, her brother became more wide-eyed and grave. Her story over, she searched his face anxiously. "Do you believe me, John?"

"Yes. Yes, I do. For a start, not even you could invent something like that. It must be true. No wonder you were so white. Who was this bloke who came to the rescue?"

"I don't know. He wouldn't say much, and he kept dodging my questions." She bit her lip. "I'm not even sure that he's human."

It was John's turn to involuntarily raise his voice. "What? Not human? What do you mean?" He stared at her.

"His eyes – I thought at first he was blind, but he's not. In fact, I think he can see better than we can. They're green, dark green, all over. There aren't any whites to them. You know what a horse's eyes look like? Well, they're something like that, only green."

John was speechless for a long moment. Then, "Come on," he said. "Get dressed."

"What for? Do you know what the time is?"

"Course I do. We've got an appointment to keep, remember? With the dwarf. I've been debating whether or not we should go, but after what you've just told me . . . we just have to get to the bottom of it."

Less than ten minutes later they were out of the house and into the half light of the new morning.

"You're up some early!" Ben stood in the doorway of the milking shed, and they could just hear the low hum of the milking machines.

"Morning, Ben," said John, lightly. "Can we go for a ride before breakfast?"

"You must be ravin' mad," the farmer chuckled. "Look at the time! Still, I suppose anythin' goes when you're on holiday. You'll have to catch the ponies yourselves, mind. Just don't be late for breakfast, else you'll 'ave Nellie clucking at 'ee. On the other hand," he added, looking at his watch, "that still gives 'ee a good two hours. Mad!" He retreated into the milking shed, shaking his head with amused disbelief.

They rode along the silent road to Treen and down a muddy

lane to the cliff path. The dark, pinnacled bulk of Treryn Dinas rose grandly from the restless sea and, at its foot, the wreck of the *Marcel Brieux* had already been broken in two. The foreshore was strewn with debris of all kinds: planking, lifebelts, splintered fittings.

They tethered the ponies in the outer ditch of the cliff castle where the turf was lush enough for them to graze, and made their way down the steep slope to the neck of the headland. Passing through the stone-lined gate of the fortress's innermost rampart, they climbed into the narrow gap between the giant crags. There, overlooking the mass of the Logan Rock, they found a place among the rocks to sit and wait, sheltered from the chill of the dawn breeze.

As they waited, the sun slipped above the distant skyline, and the grey sea turned suddenly to silver, flooding the world with new light. It was a magical scene, and they gasped at the awesome beauty of it.

"A moment of true majesty," said a solemn voice above them, "and one I never tire of seeing." It was Gawen, squatting cross-legged on a rock.

"Where did you come from?" exclaimed John, startled.

The dwarf chuckled, but let the question pass. "You are punctual," he said approvingly. "So, come. We have much to discuss and, by my reckoning, only just more than an hour and a half sunders you from breakfast."

They stared blankly at him. "How on earth did you know that?" said Penny.

The dwarf gave a great shout of laughter. "I was at your farm even as you left," he replied. "I followed you here."

He led them down to the foot of the rock-pile on which balanced the Logan Stone, and took a narrow path under its eastern side. On one hand, the cliff fell vertically away to the sea far below while, on the other, crag upon crag towered up in grotesque and curious shapes. The path came to a dead end at the foot of a steep wall of rock. The dwarf stopped and pressed his right hand against the rough stone. An irregular section of rock swung silently back, revealing a dim passage which led away into darkness.

Gawen spoke gently as John and Penny hung back, afraid. "None need fear the halls of Castle Treryn, save those with evil in their hearts. Safe you shall enter, and safe shall you return. This is the solemn promise of Gawen, son of Gwalchmai."

They followed him inside, but spun round in alarm as the granite door closed silently behind them. The dwarf reassured them again and led them on into the heart of the headland.

The passage was not as dark as they had first thought, but lit by brands fixed to the walls. At one point, it opened into a vast, dark cavern where the path led on over a high, slim bridge of rock. There were no handrails, but Gawen strolled nonchalantly across, whistling softly to himself.

John and Penny followed nervously. Far below, they could hear the sea slopping and sucking eerily in the black depths, but then they were over and entering another passage.

It was then that they heard the music. It was distant and echoed strangely through the caverns. The words of the song were too indistinct for them to make out, but the melody soared to hill-tops of joy and swooped into deep valleys of despair.

"Who is that singing?" Penny whispered. "It's beautiful!"

Gawen turned, a mildly amused look on his bearded face. "The singer is no stranger to you, maiden."

"The man who saved me from the hunters? Then he really does live here?"

"Live here? Corantyn son of Farinmail is Lord of Castle Treryn. Some name him Nadelek – in your tongue, Christmas – for such was the day of his birth. But you err in calling him Man."

"Not a man?" John exclaimed.

"Corantyn Nadelek is the last of his kind to remain in Belerion, which is the olden name for this far western part of Cornwall; or as we call it, Kernyw. His is an ancient race, a forgotten race, the eldest of peoples. By the standards of men, he is old beyond belief, yet by those of his own people he is still young.

"I have told you that he was born on the day you call Christmas, and I tell you truly 'twas on the selfsame day the Christos himself drew his first breath."

43

They looked disbelievingly at him. "You're saying he's nearly two thousand years old?" said Penny. "But he can't be. I've seen him; he's quite young."

"Age changes his kind but little. There is death for them in sickness or war, but rarely in age as there is for you. Aye, as there is for we dwarfs. I am but a third of his age and am halfway and more through my natural span."

The torchlit passage went on, twisting and turning through the jointed granite until it finally opened into a spacious cavern, lit by beams of sunlight which streamed in through chinks high in the right hand wall. The sides of this cavern were bedecked with swords, spears and shields, all gleaming as if brand-new, but their design betrayed their immense age.

On one wall hung a large tapestry, totally unlike any woven by mankind; its figures and landscapes, all in shimmering colours, seemed almost alive,and a narrative flowed in a totally unfamiliar script.

Here at last was the source of the song. At the far end of the cavern a fur-lined shelf had been cut into the rock and on this the singer half lay, half sat. One knee was drawn up and against it rested a small, exquisite harp plucked sensitively by long, graceful fingers. The singer's head bowed over the harp so that a curtain of silver-gold hair concealed his face. He sang in a language John had never before heard, but Penny recognised its long vowels and curious stresses from the previous night, when it had been spoken to calm and comfort the terrified horses.

The song came to an end, and the singer absently plucked a few extra chords before setting the harp aside. Then, in an easy, flowing movement, he swung off the seat and stood to face them. Even though he had been given ample warning, John could not suppress a gasp as he caught sight of those dark, blank eyes.

"Welcome to the halls of Castle Treryn," said the singer. "I doubt not that Gawen has told you my name, but little else. I will tell you that I have waged war with my conscience throughout this past night, for my people have little cause to love human-kind. As they have poisoned the fields and the rivers and the very air we breathe, so have they caused the decline of my people. Mine is a dying race. So few and scattered are we that men have dubbed us the Small People and today they even forget the meaning of that name and imagine us to be of tiny stature. We willingly withdrew from their sight, so that they now hold our memory in contempt and disbelief; a tale for children to marvel at.

"Yet despite all this, I feel bound in honour to aid you in whatever way I can, if only for the reason of your lineage. As to myself; I am Corantyn, by some called Nadelek, Prince of the Coraneid, that you would call the Elvish race, and I am the last of that race in Belerion."

7: THE WITCH-LORD

THE strange eyes turned to Penny. "I meant no offence in saying so little to you last evening, but there was much that was then unclear to me. Then Gawen came to me and we spoke throughout the night. Our discussion cast much light on the matter." He motioned them to a fur-lined couch cut into the cave wall, much like his own. "This much is clear," he continued. "There is a mind at work against you; the mind of a man of fearsome power. Marek, Lord of Pengersek, whom we believed long dead."

The tall elf paused while Gawen served them pleasant drinks in ornate goblets. Then he returned to his own seat, stretching out and plucking thoughtfully at a harpstring.

"Behind every man," he said, "there lies a story, and so it is with this man. I will make it as brief as I can, for the full tale is long, filled with plottings, witchcraft and murder; crimes more terrible than you could dream of. But the story should be told, for it is meet that you should know your enemy.

"The tale begins many centuries ago, on the shores of Mount's Bay. In a wooded vale by the beach of Praa Sands stands Pengersek Castle. That which stands today is the second such building on the site; it is to the first that this tale belongs.

"The father of our enemy was guilty of such crimes that my

heart quails at the memory of them, but his son, Marek – which in the Old Tongue means 'horseman' – grew to be of goodly character and appearance. True to his name, he became a master horseman and hunter. Few were the sports at which he did not excel, and his singing and harp-play were second to none. He was a young man who, when the occasion arose, would willingly risk his own life to save those of shipwrecked mariners.

"Into the garden of his life there entered a serpent, in the guise of Engrina, a lady of Godolphin. She was infatuated with Marek, and more so with the prospect of his rich inheritance. But she was far older than he and Marek firmly, but politely, rebuffed her advances. She persevered, even resorting to witchcraft in order to ensnare him, but all her plans went awry.

"Still she was not to be thwarted, and she contrived to wed the old lord, whose own wife was long dead. Engrina would stop at nothing to gain the inheritance of the Pengersek estate and fortune, only Marek stood in her way. Thus, she set to work in poisoning the old man's mind against his son.

"In this she succeeded, and the old lord arranged for Moorish pirates to seize Marek and to sell him into slavery, but timely word reached Marek's ear. He escaped and fled Cornwall, travelling across the seas to the land of the Saracens. There, he heard of sages who dwelt on a distant mountain; men who were masters of the arts of magic. For many years he studied under them and so thoroughly did he absorb their teachings that even they began to fear his powers.

"Some years later, on learning of his father's death, Marek returned unexpectedly to Pengersek Castle. He brought with him his wife, a Saracen lady of noble blood, and two servants. All rode the magnificent horses of Araby, children of the south wind, and all spoke in a strange tongue. Marek's own steed was a mare of the deepest black; so fiery that none but he could control her. Some held that this was no earthly horse, but a base demon in horse-shape, a familiar bound in the service of the sorcerer.

"Marek found Engrina in the cellars of the castle. She was horribly deformed, the result of inhaling the foul brews of witchcraft that had obsessed her. When she saw that Marek had returned, she fled the castle and flung herself from the cliffs.

"This new lord was much changed from the Marek of old. Perhaps the reason lay in his treatment at the hands of his father and stepmother; perhaps the power of the sorcery he had learned had distorted his mind; perhaps the evil of the father had always been inherent in the son. Most likely, it was a blend of all three, but Pengersek Castle became a place of terror for the countryfolk as the sorcerer, the Witch-Lord, wrestled and fought in his tower to gain mastery over the demons he conjured from the pit, and as he strove to unlock the secrets of alchemy.

"He made many discoveries, perhaps the greatest of which was that of an Elixir of Life which both he and his lady regularly consumed."

The elf looked up and gazed at John and Penny, who had followed the strange tale without a murmur.

"It is this part of Pengersek's life, this elixir, which Gawen and I believe is the key to what is now taking place. But hear the rest of the tale before I explain further.

"Protected from both age and death by this elixir of life, Pengersek and his lady lived far beyond the span of mortal men, but the time came when the lady of Pengersek began to tire of outliving her children and grandchildren. She drank no more of the life-giving fluid and quickly found the death she desired.

"Pengersek became a fury, a figure of terror as he strove to find new power, new wealth and, above all, a new partner. In so doing, he came across the only man ever to defeat him, a wandering prospector for tin who had set up home with a local chieftain and desired to marry his daughter. But this was the girl on whom Pengersek had set his eyes. He underestimated the prospector – but that is another tale for another time. Suffice it to say that Pengersek was defeated and fled back to the safety of his tower.

"Soon after this, a stranger appeared in the town of Marghas-vyghan, opposite the Mount. He was young and bronzed of skin. From whence he came, no man knew. He spoke to no one, sought neither food nor wine, lodging nor company, but some said that he was oft to be seen of a moonlit night, seated on a rock and gazing down on Pengersek Castle.

"Then, one stormy night, a fearful crash was heard and a fiery glow appeared in the sky. Pengersek Castle was ablaze and, by morning, had burned to the ground. No trace of the Witch-Lord's body was ever found and, from that night, none saw the young stranger ever again.

"Many believed that this had been Satanas, the Dark One, in earthly form, come to claim that which was long overdue: the soul of Pengersek. All believed that Pengersek had gone forever and today, as I have said, another castle stands on the spot. Men preserved the sorcerer's memory when they renamed Pengersek Cove, Porth Wragh – the Witch's Cove – though they shorten it now to Praa.

"Now we see that Pengersek did not meet with his fate on that terrible night. Perhaps the fire was a ruse of his own to confound the Dark One, for the Witch-Lord still lives. This I know, for I have seen him."

Penny sat up with a start. "Still alive? But how?"

Corantyn's mouth curled up slightly at the corners. "As he has always survived, by courtesy of his elixir. I would guess that he has been lurking in the Saracen mountains where he learned his art, but now he is once more in his native land. Something has drawn him back."

He propped his harp against the wall, swung his long legs from the seat and walked slowly down the great cavern. He stopped about halfway and pointed to a large, squarish boss of rock which projected from the wall.

The face of the protruding rock had been carved into the shape of a circular shield, pierced through by a sculpted sword so that hilt and point stood out above and below. The centre of the shield was inscribed with words similar in appearance to those on the tapestry opposite, forming two verses, beneath which were the letters M A, each twined into the other.

"This is written in the Old Tongue," said Corantyn, "and was carved here fifteen centuries ago by one of the greatest prophets and bards of the island of Britain, who once dwelt here at Castle Treryn.

"This was a prophecy for this farthest point of Cornwall and is thus known as the Belerion Prophecy. You can be sure the Witch-Lord knows it well, for I believe that it, too, has much to do with his return. In your own tongue, it says this:

'In days ever strange to the cry of the horn
Shall times intermingle and bright shine a Stone.
Two innocent ones, of a midsummer morn
Shall unlock the portals, old memories be known,
A Raven be summoned, and fires greet the sun.
By the Dark Hour of Witchcraft shall these deeds be done.'

"So runs the first of the verses. The words, of course, are cryptic, but the Stone that shall shine is surely that which you now wear."

Penny's hand flew to the green gem in her pendant. "The Crownstone? But why?"

"Have you not already found that the Crownstone of Lyonesse is much more than it seems? As its power protected the Lords of Lyonesse, so it protects their descendants, and thus it came to your aid in your hour of need. That apart, the power of the stone is largely a law unto itself, as it demonstrated at the circle of Boscawen-ûn.

"Remember the words inscribed here: 'Bright shine a Stone. Two innocent ones, of a midsummer morn, Shall unlock the portals, Old memories be known.' Is this not what occurred yesterday, and is not the Eve of Golowan, Midsummer Eve, just two days hence?

"What the stone has so far shown you is but a fraction of its true power, one that is rare in the world of today. This is what draws Pengersek. He craves the power locked within that jewel, and it takes little to guess his purpose.

"For centuries, his elixir has kept him both alive and young, but his life can only last for as long as he can find the ingredients of the liquid. What he seeks is true immortality. Only then can he become the figure of power he desires to be; not only within this world, but beyond it. There is no doubt that the forces of the Crownstone can be turned to this purpose, if one knows the method; and I fear that the arts of the Witch-Lord are capable of this."

Gawen, who up to now had been content to listen, stroked his beard pensively. "It is just two nights since I sensed that evil was waking again in this land," he said. "I was to the north of here, hard by the Hooting Carn. It is long since that hill lived up to its ill repute, but on that night its voices were in full cry, as of old. By daybreak, it was silent again and I considered it safe to go there, to seek the reason. I found no answer, nor any clue. Later that morning, I chanced upon the tinner, who told me of the Witch-Lord's return, and so I came south to speak with Corantyn of it. From the rocks of Creeg Tol, I saw the circle of Boscawen-ûn, its dragon-breath alive, and the guilty ones – innocent ones – creeping away."

"And all because of this," Penny muttered, cupping the Crownstone in her hand. "Perhaps it would be better if I threw it back in the sea where it came from."

"And what would that solve?" said Corantyn, "it has found you once; it would find you again. If not yourselves, then your children, or their children. Pengersek would wait, be it another thousand years. You cannot destroy it, nor can you send it away for, wherever it went, he would surely follow."

"In other words," said Penny, "I'm stuck with it."

"A choice that is not a choice," the elf replied, "but you will not face what is to come alone. Both Gawen and I have pledged our aid, and there is good reason why we, too, wish to keep the Witch-Lord from succeeding in his quest for immortality."

"I don't quite understand why you're so willing to help us," John broke in. "You said yourself that you don't like the human race, so what makes us different?"

Corantyn gazed at each of them in turn. "It is because the blood of my people flows in your veins. By his father, the Lord Trevelyan was human, but his mother was elvish. Therefore, you yourselves carry the blood of the Half-Elven."

It took a moment or two for these words to sink in and it was John who recovered first. "This Witch-Lord, Pengersek," he said, "How would we know him if we saw him?"

"But you have already seen him. Think, who has shown an undue interest in the Stone? Do you know a man who rides a coal-black mare?"

Penny's mouth fell open. "Henry Milliton! He was asking me about the Stone in the village, and I began to feel faint. That was when he had that argument with the vicar."

"Ha!" barked Gawen. "Is that what he calls himself? I think, Corantyn, that the conjurer lacks originality. Even a false name fails to conceal him."

The elf explained. "Pengersek has hidden himself behind a name he has taken from both his father, Henry of Pengersek, and John Milliton, who built the castle that stands today."

"What can we do about him?" John asked.

"There is little you can do on your own," answered the elf, "save to avoid him as best you can. We need time in which to devise the means to confound him. I wonder, Gawen, if the tinner would be willing to help? What think you?"

John and Penny puzzled silently at this question as Gawen replied to it. "Perhaps. Perhaps not. He is his own master, but it will do no harm to ask him. If, that is, we can find him."

Corantyn nodded briefly and turned back to John and Penny. "Then that must be the first move for Gawen and myself. When we have news, we will bring it to you. Until then, take great care; and be sure that you are within doors between sunset and sunrise. We know that the Nôshelyas serve the Witch-Lord, but it is at night that they walk abroad. Pengersek will be reluctant, to act alone, and he will be careful. He knows of the protective powers of the Crownstone, and he fears it as much as he craves it.

"Now, you must return to Trehelya Vean before anxieties are raised. Remember, when we have news, you will hear of it."

He began to lead them back along the cavern, but John paused to look again at the mysterious carved prophecy and the entwined letters beneath.

"M A," he read aloud. "Were those the prophet's initials?"

"Indeed they were," replied Corantyn, "and you, of all people, have the right to see the greatest secret of Castle Treryn. Come."

He led them into a dim side passage, cut in the heart of the rock. At its end there hung a heavy curtain of the deepest blue. The elf reached out and drew it back. Behind, a small alcove was lit by four candles on tall iron stands, and it held a great tomb of wrought granite. The tomb itself was bare and plain, except for the side facing them. In the centre of this was a finely carved face.

It was the face of an elderly, full-bearded man, hook-nosed and wide of brow. Flowing hair, frozen in stone, fell from the sides of a bald, domed pate, and the eyes were closed. There was wisdom and sadness in the face and a deep serenity. Below the carving were the same entwined letters: M A.

Corantyn kept his voice low and solemn. "Here you see the tomb of a great one; magician, bard and prophet, who was once imprisoned in these caverns by the wiles of an enchantress. Later, and by his own arts, he freed himself, but he knew that his place in the world was over. His heart lay here at Castle Treryn, and he wished it to be his home during his final years. This I was right glad to grant, for I was lord here even then, though mostly in absence. Those were the dark years for Britain, and I spent much time fighting alongside my father and the British kings against the Saxon invaders.

"The man who now lies here lived to a great age, and the strength and power of his mind was such that it could have lived for ever. His body, though, was mortal and frail, and could not resist the inevitability of death. Here we laid him to rest and his monument was the great rocking stone above us which men now call the Logan Stone, but was then named, after him, Mên Amber.

"In the Old Tongue, the name of this man was Merthen Emrys, but to you, and to the world, he is known and famed as Merlin Ambrosius."

8: STONE OF WRITING

THE engine house of the tin mine, high on a moorland ridge, was an empty sentinel guarding the bleak landscape. Around it lay pits and mounds, the ravages of a long-dead industry. Now, nature had returned, filling the pits and cloaking the mounds with brambles as though seeking to cover its disfigurement.

The building itself was a shell of granite, with a slim chimney pointing to the sky. Empty windows stared out across the wasteland and over fields and woods to the sea and the grey pile of St Michael's Mount rising from the bay. A breeze soughed through the deserted building and birds sang from the tops of its walls. It was a peaceful place.

John wriggled uncomfortably in his saddle and groped for the guide book. "This is the Greenburrow Stack of Ding Dong Mine," he announced. "So I reckon we head north from here."

Penny frowned in suspicion. "What are you up to?"

He grinned impishly. "I'm on the lookout for things called 'carns'."

"What are they, when they're at home?"

"Outcrops of rock on the tops of hills, like tors on Dartmoor; only here they can be on cliff tops as well. I asked Ben. Remember when Corantyn and Gawen were talking this morning? Well, Gawen mentioned a place called the Hooting Carn, somewhere to the north of Treryn Dinas. I can't find any such place on the map, so it might have another name, and I thought we might have a look around."

Penny turned on him angrily. "Is that why you've led us all the way up here? John, you idiot! Gawen said the Hooting Carn was an evil place!"

"Oh, come on, Penny, it's broad daylight," he said defensively. "Nothing's going to happen to us in broad daylight. They said so, didn't they?"

"No, they didn't. They told us not to go out at night, but that doesn't mean we can be careless at other times. Anyway, what about Boscawen-ûn? That was in broad daylight, wasn't it?"

"Yes, but that wasn't exactly evil, was it? It didn't hurt us. Just gave us a bit of a scare, that's all."

"But you heard what Gawen said. Both good and evil forces were set off!" Penny rolled up her eyes in exasperation. "Anyway, as you're so clever, how do you know if the Hooting Carn's on a hill or a cliff?"

"You weren't listening, were you?" came the smug reply. "Gawen said quite clearly that it was on a hill." Feeling that he'd won the point, John pointed to the north where a huge peak bared a trio of jagged teeth at the sky. "There are any number of places called Carn something on the map. That's Carn Galva, and just east of it is a place called Hannibal's Carn. I don't think it'll hurt to take a look . . . from a distance, anyway."

Penny looked unhappy. "Well, all right. Just so long as it is from a distance."

A well-worn path led north from the mine track near the engine house, towards the massive outcrop a mile or so away. It left the mine-ravaged area and its deep shafts, entering unspoilt, boulder-studded moorland. This was rising country, and the soft ground showed that horses had passed this way many times.

Penny looked across the bleak landscape, and noticed a curious arrangement of stones which was almost camouflaged in the rugged surroundings. She shivered involuntarily as a chill swept through her.

"John." Her voice sounded dull and lifeless. "Look, there's another stone circle here."

"So there is," he said, following her gaze. "Fancy building one here! It's in the middle of nowhere." He glanced round and saw the troubled look on his sister's face. "Don't worry, we'll be all right. Look at it; it's a ruin. At least half the stones are missing. If this one ever had the sort of power we saw at Boscawen-ûn, it must have lost it years ago."

The circle had certainly seen better days. Only eleven stones remained from perhaps nineteen, and four of those lay flat and forlorn. Of the other seven, two or three leaned outward at alarming angles. One of the stones which still stood upright, and flanked by two fallen ones, was unusually tall: nearly seven feet high.

"I still don't like it," Penny muttered. "It's got that same sort of feeling about it as Boscawen-ûn, ruined or not." Instinctively, she glanced down at the Crownstone. Was there just the tiniest hint of a gleam deep in the heart of the jewel; a minute flame of ice-cold emerald? She decided not. It was only, perhaps, a reflection of sunlight.

The fact that she was, at that moment facing north did not occur to her. The Crownstone lay in her shadow.

They rode on at a canter, past the stone circle and the stump of a broken menhir, to the highest part of the ridge. Here, by the path, was a line of ancient barrows. Two of these were little more than low, grassy humps, while the third, the largest, had disintegrated, leaving a ring of inward leaning stones which had once been part of the wall retaining the old burial mound. They reined in beside it and gazed across the sweep of moorland to the towers of Carn Galva's southern peak.

"I don't think that's your Hooting Carn," said Penny. "It doesn't feel evil."

John pondered the fact that he would have ridiculed a statement like that had it been made a day or two earlier. "No," he agreed. "It doesn't."

He turned his head to take another look at the stone circle behind them, then looked back again at the magnificence of Carn Galva. He blinked in delayed surprise and looked back again at the circle, but all seemed normal enough. Yet he would have sworn that, at the first glance, the circle had stood complete, with all nineteen stones in place and upright. He shook his head: the recent weird events were getting to him. He looked a third time, just to be absolutely sure, but there was only a ruined and incomplete circle with stones upright, fallen, leaning, missing.

Amd yet something had quietly crept into the scene; something invisible and intangible. The air had stilled and the sky was darkening over the moor. Before the clouds which swept in from the west, the shadows fled.

Some way to their left, about four hundred yards away and in the centre of a small, triangular field, there rose a tall stone of unhewn granite. Its name was Mên Scryfa, which meant: Stone of Writing.

Even as the clouds banked up, a voice rose from the empty desolation around them, whispering and hollow. They could not tell from whence it came and somehow it seemed part of the unearthly stillness. It was a song; an eerie refrain which circled in the air like the flight of a falcon. The words came clearly to their ears, words they had heard once before:

> "In days ever strange to the cry of the horn
> Shall times intermingle and bright shine a Stone.
> Two innocent ones, of a midsummer morn,
> Shall unlock the portals, old memories be known.
> A Raven be summoned . . ."

The words tailed off, leaving the verse unfinished, and the tone changed to a higher, more commanding one. Now it was calling, and their spines chilled to the sound of it.

"Rialobran . . . Rialobran, Royal Raven, son of Cunoval King. The verse of the prophet calls to thee as written long ago. Awake, Rialobran! Come forth from thy stone, O great and mighty Prince of warriors!"

There was a long moment of utter silence. Then, a second voice replied to the first, a rich, noble voice which seemed to issue from the very earth itself.

"Rialobran map Cunoval has woken, and heeds the call of the prophet. Darkness falls once more upon Belerion. I rise against the Darkness, and the Shadows shall flee from my wrath!"

The strangeness of it all was frightening, yet the children found they could not move. The ground around the base of the lonely standing stone was beginning to exude tendrils of white mist that meshed and thickened, to form a globe enveloping the ageless Stone of Writing, while at its heart a shape was forming. An unseen horse gave voice to a mighty cry, filled with joy, which echoed round and around the silent hills. Their ponies jerked up their heads at the sound, ears pricked and eyes gleaming, and whinnied in response.

Out of the ghostly mist rode a horseman. Even at that distance and in the gloom of the cloud, they could see that he rode a majestic horse of the purest white and that he wore a cloak of deep purple, the colour of kings. Mail glimmered beneath its folds. A circlet lay upon his brow, his dark hair was long and wild and a great moustache swept down and back to the line of his jaw. Perhaps it was a trick of the light, but both horse and rider seemed to be of unnatural size.

The great horse reared, welcoming the world, and at the same moment, its rider noticed the watchers on the ridgetop. He drew his sword, and a stray beam of sunlight flashed on the broad blade as he raised the hilt to his lips in salute. Then, sheathing the sword in a single, smooth movement, he urged the horse on.

They continued to watch in silence, as the warrior rode away to the east, following the path of a long forgotten ridgeway track. He passed between the children and the dark rock called Little Galva, before descending into the Bosporthennis valley. Minutes later, he reappeared far away near the ruined Stone Age tomb on the crest of Mulfra Hill, then he vanished over its brow and beyond their sight.

John and Penny stared, speechless, at each other; then John abruptly kicked his pony on, his eyes fixed on the Stone of Writing. Penny hesitated for a moment, before following nervously. Above them, the clouds began to break up and disperse.

The Mên Scryfa stood clear again of its misty shroud, of which not a trace remained. They dismounted and entered the field in which it stood. John began to study it. It was a rough pillar of granite, the height of a tall man, and set solidly in the ground, but it bore that same aura of ancient mystery that they

Out of the ghostly mist rode a horseman

had felt at the two stone circles. He walked around it shrugging his shoulders.

"There's nothing all that special . . ." He stopped, bent quickly, and his fingers reached out to trace something incised in the uneven surface of the stone.

Penny's expression was strained. "What is it? What have you found?"

John looked up slowly. "That voice – it called out a name. Can you remember?"

She frowned, searching her memory. "A strange name. Something like – Rialobran? Yes, that's it, Rialobran – and something about a Royal Raven, son of some king or other. Cuno-something, I think. Why d'you ask?"

John stood up and pointed at the stone. Penny came round to look. Running down the northern face of the standing stone, in two rows, were three carved words:

RIALOBRAN

CYNOVAL-FIL-

"No!" Penny cried the word out loud. "It can't be! It can't have been him!"

John set his jaw. "Why not? He appeared out of nowhere, didn't he? You saw how he was dressed! And that sword!" His eyes betrayed his fear. "What's happening to us? First dwarves, then elves, then those night-riders of yours. Now it's ghosts – in broad daylight!"

"No, John," said Penny quietly, looking at the ground. The chill had crept back into her body. "Not a ghost. Whatever we've just seen, it wasn't a ghost." Her shaking finger pointed.

There in the turf, beginning at the foot of the Stone of Writing, and leading away eastward, was a deeply impressed trail of immense hoofprints.

9: THE HOOTING CARN

"HEY!" John's sudden cry startled Penny, whose mind was elsewhere. "It's in here." His reins angled over his pony's neck, leaving it free to pick its own way down the stony track while he riffled through the pages of his guide book.

"What is?" Apprehension quivered in her voice. "You haven't found that Hooting Carn, have you? Do leave it alone; we're in deep enough trouble as it is."

"No, not that," he said. "The stone with the writing on it. Listen. It's called the Mên Scryfa, and the words on it say: 'Rialobran, son of Cunoval'. According to this, they're Celtic names which mean 'Royal Raven' and 'Powerful Chieftain.' It's a sixth-century memorial to a local hero, a warrior prince 'who was slain near the spot in single combat against an unknown enemy. Legend says that the overall length of the stone, more than eight feet, equalled the height of the slain warrior'."

"The sixth century?" asked Penny. "Isn't that when the Lyonesse was destroyed, and when the prophecy was made?"

Her brother frowned. "So it is. I wonder if there's a connection?"

"I don't care if there is,"she retorted. "I just want to get as far away from here as I can. I don't suppose you've got any idea where we are?"

"As a matter of fact, I have, 'cause the Mên Scryfa's marked on the map. If we carry on down this lane and cross the road at the bottom, it'll lead us to a castle. That has to be worth a look before we head for home."

"And end up in even more trouble, I suppose."

"If you are going to look at things like that," said John, "we could get into trouble anywhere, couldn't we?"

THE hill was coated in heather and dwarf Western gorse, but a worn path, marked by a whitewashed boulder, led to the summit.

"I don't see any castle." Penny looked accusingly at her brother. "I bet you've got it wrong again."

"No, I haven't. I've been right so far. Anyway, there was a notice at the farm down there which said 'Chûn Castle!" He sat up in his saddle. "Wait a minute, though. What's this?"

Rising from the gorse on the hill-top was a wall, overgrown and about seven feet high. Here and there, heavy stonework showed through the bracken. They found the remains of an entrance and, leaving the ponies to graze, walked through to find themselves confronted by a second wall. This was virtually free of vegetation but, although built of massive stones, was hardly taller than the outer wall. The way through was a tapering gateway flanked by two tall stones. Between the walls were lesser ruins which suggested that the staggered entrance had been cunningly designed. The inner wall was incredibly thick; fifteen feet or more, but it was obvious that a lot of its stone had been carted away, probably to build barns and walls. It was now a great ring of tumbled granite blocks with little of its vertical facings visible. Inside were signs that buildings had stood against this huge wall and a well, now choked with stone, still had a glint of water at the bottom. They could see that the pair of concentric walls encircled the hill-top and that the whole structure was about a hundred yards across.

"Is this it?" Penny looked puzzled. "It doesn't look much like a castle to me."

John's nose was back between the pages of his book. "Chûn Castle . . . yes, here it is." He whistled softly. "No wonder it's in this state. Do you know how old it is?"

She shook her head. "I haven't a clue."

"It was built in the third century BC. It's an Iron Age hill fort and . . . "

"And what?"

"It was re-used during – "

"The sixth century." Penny completed the sentence for him. "That's enough for me. I'm going!"

John followed her back to where the ponies were contentedly cropping the short grass on the footpath. "What's that?" he said suddenly. "That stone thing over there?"

A few hundred yards away, lower down the western slope of the hill, stood a curious object. Four large slabs, each about five feet high and leaning inwards against each other, formed a rough box which was covered by an enormous capstone some ten feet or so square. The base of the structure was embedded in the remains of a stony mound. It looked for all the world like a colossal, squat mushroom.

"Chûn Quoit," said John, running his finger down the page. "The book reckons it might be as much as five thousand years old."

"What was it?" asked Penny. "Does it say?"

"Yes, it's a Stone Age tomb."

She pulled a face. "I wish I hadn't asked now."

But John wasn't listening. Something on the map caught his eye and he glanced up at the western skyline. Across a flat stretch of moor, closed in on three sides by hills, rose a shallow peak capped by a massive formation of rock. Even in sunlight it looked strangely menacing; brooding and sinister. John flicked his way to the index, found the right page and ran his eye over it.

"Rising above the weirdly flat tract of moor called The Gump," he read, "are the rocks of Carn Kenidzhek, or Kenidjack as it is now more commonly spelt. In legend, this is the notorious Hooting Carn, haunt of ghosts and demon-wrestlers, where the Devil rides a black horse at the dead of night in pursuit of lost souls." John's eyes lit up as he crammed the book back in his pocket.

"Come on!" he shouted, climbing onto his pony and setting off at a canter.

"Now what? John, wait for me!"

"There!" he called back, pointing excitedly at the distant rocks. "That's it! The Hooting Carn!"

Penny raced her pony after him, finally catching him up halfway along the rough track which skirted the edge of The Gump. "John, slow up!"

He reined back, impatiently.

"I don't want to go up there," she said. "I don't like the look of it."

"Oh, come on," he urged. "We'll be all right! Look, I know a lot of weird things have been happening, but nothing's actually done us any harm."

"Those Night Hunters would have."

"But Corantyn said they only come out at night and it's only a quarter to three; sunset's an hour away. And isn't the Crownstone supposed to protect us? Anyway, Gawen said it was safe to go up there during daylight. It would be a shame not to look at it after coming all this way. I bet there's a super view from the top."

Unwisely, Penny refrained from saying that Gawen had not said exactly that, but she knew that in his present mood John would not have listened.

JOHN was right about the view from the crag. It was breathtaking. The boulder- strewn hill-side fell away to the south and west to the mottled greens in the valley. Two miles away, the small town of St Just perched on the valley side and, far away out to sea, creamy foam surged at the wicked reef around the tower of the Longships Lighthouse, off the Land's End itself.

It was pleasant to sit on the great carn. soaking up the scenery and the sun while the ponies grazed below, but the afternoon was slipping away and they had to keep an eye on the time. Now that they were actually there, the weird shapes of the outcrop seemed to lose their sinister aspect. The granite was warm under the rays of the sun, and welcoming, but it was time to head for home. They scrambled down from the rocks and onto the springy heather.

In an instant, a second mist clamped down on them; warm

sunshine had turned to a cold, impenetrable murk, and they instinctively knew that it was not natural.

"Where did it come from?" Penny whispered.

"I don't know. There wasn't a sign of it a moment ago. Stay close to me, we mustn't get separated. How are we going to find the ponies? I can't see a thing . . . What's that?"

From the depths of the gloom rose a low moan. It grew louder, increasing in pitch, and came to an end with a blood-curdling hoot. A second joined it, from a different direction, then another and another, until the entire murky world was filled with the hideous sounds. The children turned this way and that, desperately seeking any sign of the ponies, but could see nothing in the swirling curtain of grey.

Penny screamed. John whirled and saw a look of horror and revulsion in her eyes, but too late to see what she had seen. "There!" she wailed, "That horrible thing!" She pointed wildly, but there was only mist.

For the briefest of instants, a tongue of mist had folded back to unveil the most repulsive creature she had ever seen or even dreamed of. It crouched on a ledge above her, peering balefully down with yellow, cat-like eyes. Beneath a thin hook of a nose, with high-arching nostrils, a great gash of a mouth leered hideously, and thin, furrowed lips were drawn back over sharp, discoloured teeth. It was man-like, but it was not a man: the large head, with its high, pointed ears, and its wasted body, covered with wrinkled skin, were completely hairless. It squatted with claw-nailed hands spread out on the rock beside its splayed feet as though it were about to spring. Then, mercifully, the mist swirled back to hide the ghastly thing.

"Run for it!" barked John.

"But the ponies – Which way?"

"I don't know! Just run – and hang on to me!"

They ran, pounding over the heather; tripping, falling, scrambling up and running again. They could see no more than a few yards in the murk, but then a rough path appeared at their feet and the dim shapes of stone hedges to either side.

"It's the lane!" John panted. "The one we came up just now. It'll lead us to the road."

They fled down the track, splashing ankle-deep through muddy puddles and stumbling over loose stones. At last they reached the road. But there was still no respite, no shelter. The howling fog was moving with them, keeping them at its heart.

"Now which way?" Penny's breath came in gasps, more from fear than fatigue.

"Left. No, right; go right! It leads south, towards home!"

They scurried on, the sounds of their racing feet and laboured breath lost in the terrible howls and shrieks surrounding them. John skidded to a sudden stop. "Wait a minute . . . this isn't the road."

They stood at the foot of a steep stony track which faded into the gloom. John began to think, his fright giving way to reason. Whatever it was that lurked in the mist had yet to show any real sign of doing more than frightening them. It was more as if . . . yes, that was it! They were being driven; herded like sheep. But to where? Or to whom?

They were completely lost. Neither had the slightest clue in what direction the track led, except that it went uphill. John made up his mind. "Come on, we'll follow it."

On they ran, up the track which got steeper all the time. Penny felt her legs faltering. The mind willed the body on, but her strength was limited. She cried out in desperation, "John, I can't go on much further!"

He stopped, knowing that he hadn't the strength left to haul her up the hill. The inhabitants of the mist sensed victory. The hellish row suddenly increased fourfold, triumphant – and as quickly broke off, sinking into a babble of uncertainty and confusion.

Something was coming down the lane towards them. John stiffened, moving protectively in front of his sister. At first, he saw no more than a dim shape, without detail, but it was a man. Or was it?

The figure was of medium height and strode purposefully on. One arm was upraised, as if holding something above his head.

His head -

From the top of the head curved two great horns, sweeping upward at their tips. John's mouth dropped open and his knees

"All your noise and ugly faces can't harm an honest tinner!"

turned to water. Penny let out a sob of fear and crumpled into a fainting heap.

The horned figure marched closer, then, through the murk, a voice rang out: "Howl away, devils! All your noise and ugly faces can't harm an honest tinner!"

10: AN HONEST TINNER

PENNY woke to the soft snuffle of a grazing horse, and the warm caress of sunlight on her cheek. She blinked and looked up, to see the granite walls and chimney of a derelict engine house looming above her. It seemed familiar, but she did not recognise the chestnut gelding which cropped at the grass beneath the walls and there was no sign of John. She struggled to sit up for a better look.

"And about time," said a voice behind her. "I was beginning to think you were never going to wake up." It was a young man's voice, filled with life and humour. Penny turned and, for an instant, her heart leaped into her mouth. The stranger sat on a boulder, drawing calmly at a long clay pipe and puffing idle smoke-rings into the air. He was athletic in build and wore the most curious coat she had ever seen. It had been fashioned from the hide of a young bull and was covered with black curly hair. The sleeves had once been the animal's forelegs and were skilfully fashioned to fit the wearer.

"Who are you?" Penny was more curious than fearful. "Where's my brother?"

"Whoa now!" The strange figure flung up a hand in mock defence. "One thing at a time. Your brother is inside the engine house fetching something for me. He's in excellent health as you'll see for yourself in a moment. As to myself, I'm a tinner. I prospect for tin; I mine it and smelt it, and not only tin. I'll fashion any metal you care to name into anything you like. I'm a fair blacksmith, too; hence this." He patted a massive hammer that was tucked behind his belt. "I mend pots and pans, shoe horses, make tools; turn my hand to anything." He smiled. "It's a living."

"Yes," she persisted, "but you must have a name."

"Jack. That's what they call me: Jack the Tinner. Some call me Jack of the Hammer." He fondled the great hammer almost affectionately. "Here's your brother now," he added as the boy emerged from the engine house. "Did you find it, John?"

"In the end. – How on earth do you manage to pack so much stuff in a small bag like that?"

The tinner laughed. "That tool bag of mine is a legend, my lad, and I'd be a lost man without it." He took the leather flask from John, uncorked it, and raised it to his lips. "Nectar," he murmured, drawing the back of his hand across his mouth.

"Are you sure you're all right?" John asked his sister with concern. "You were out for ages."

"It seemed more than an ordinary faint," said Jack. "I should think our friends in the mist had a hand in it. It wouldn't be beyond them. Perhaps you should try a drop of this." He handed her the flask.

Penny took an exploratory sniff. "What is it?"

"It's a kind of barley wine. I brew it myself and", he added furtively, "I've a secret store. It's strong stuff, mind, but you'll feel the better for it."

She took a sip to taste then, as her eyes widened at its exquisite sweetness, took another, longer, draught.

"Hey, now!" cried the tinner. "Gently! That's powerful stuff."

Penny smiled and handed the flask on to her brother. "Where are we?" she asked.

"Ding Dong Mine," said John. "We passed it earlier, remember?"

"I remember it all right," she said accusingly. "We came to it just before you led us into all kinds of trouble!"

"I know." John's voice carried a genuine apology. "It was Jack here who got us out of it."

She looked at the bizarre figure. "How did you do it? And what were those – things?"

"Spriggans," he replied. "A goblin tribe that infests this region. Not the most cordial folk you could meet, nor the most delightful souls you ever saw."

Penny shuddered at the memory of the hideous creature that had peered sovenomously at her from the ledge on Carn Kenidjack. The tinner went on: "I know them, and how best to deal with them. Two things they fear more than anything: one is fire, the other is this."

He reached inside his coat and drew out a small disc of metallic stone. It had a hole through its centre and was attached to a leather thong which hung about his neck.

"The ironstone," he said, "is very rare but powerful. Folk would scoff at it these days, but it is proof against many forms of evil. Some think me mad, or at best eccentric, for I have never treated legend and lore with scorn. The ironstone has served me well. The spriggans cannot bear to be near it for, to them, its touch is death."

His gaze turned to Penny and the humour in his eyes faded. "It seems to me that the Crownstone of Lyonesse is leading you both a merry dance."

She gasped, taken aback by his unexpected knowledge. "How do you know about the Stone?"

"How not? Since it freed the dragon's breath from Boscawen-ûn, half Belerion knows; those who recognise such things at any rate – and their number might surprise you."

John broke in with the question which had been on his lips for some time. "Was the Crownstone responsible for making Rialobran appear?"

It was the tinner's turn to be taken by surprise and he all but choked on his pipe. Penny told him of the disembodied voice on the moor which had called the warrior from his stone.

Jack listened intently, hanging on her every word. "So the prophecy unravels line by line: 'A Raven be summoned'. If he has been called, then we are indeed in deep water. I had thought to stay out of this, but it seems I no longer can. It has become far graver that I had imagined."

"You know about the prophecy as well?" John asked.

"Of course! As I said, I do not scorn legend and lore. Instead, I make it my business to study them, and learn."

"Who is Rialobran?" Penny asked.

"Many centuries ago," said the tinner, "he was Prince of Belerion, and should have been king. He was a good man who cared for his people but, to his foes, a terrible adversary.

"After the battle of Vellan-drokkia, near St Buryan, where he aided Arthur in defeating an invasion of the Sea Wolves, Rialobran became one of Arthur's officers and fought alongside him in twelve great battles. The twelfth conflict, at Mount Badon, scattered the Saxonkind so widely that they were unable to reorganise until long after Arthur's death. At last there was some kind of peace in Britain, and Rialobran was able to return to his home, only to find that a cruel usurper had taken his lands and murdered his family. The prince was able to scrape up an army from his loyal subjects and a battle took place on the moor which is called Gûnajynyal – the downs of the desolate pass - which ended with single combat between Rialobran and the usurper himself. The prince fought bravely and fiercely, but was sorely weakened by the many wounds inflicted at Badon. He and his enemy slew each other.

"Rialobran was laid to rest, along with his warhorse, beneath the old menhir which stood close by, and on this they carved his name. It was found that the length of the stone and the height of the prince were identical, and the magicians and soothsayers took this to be a sign. They held that, like Arthur himself, Rialobran was not dead, but merely slept in readiness for the day when his land and his people were again in need of him."

From the corner of her eye, Penny saw Jack's gelding look up suddenly from his grazing, ears and eyes alert.

"Someone's coming!" she hissed, but Jack had already slid his hammer from his belt, and sat ready, weighing it in his hand

There was a whistling sound, and John and Penny shrank back as a gleaming object hurtled through the air towards them. The tinner did not move or even flinch as it half buried itself, quivering, in the turf between his feet. It was a double bladed war-axe fitted with a short, leather-bound haft.

The tinner relaxed, smiling softly, and tucked the hammer back into his belt. "Your aim improves, if slightly," he called languidly."But now you'll have to clean your axe, son of Gwalchmai."

Penny and John stared in surprise as the squat, bearded figure of Gawen strode into view. He was followed by the tall figure of Corantyn who carried his longbow on his shoulder. The elf's slanting eyebrows drew together perplexedly.

"John – Penny? How is it you are here?"

The tinner spared them the embarrassment of explaining by recounting their story himself. Corantyn's blank eyes fixed on John, who shuffled uncomfortably and looked down at his feet.

"But why should you seek the Hooting Carn?" said the elf, in a way that made John want to hide. "Or could it be that other forces drew on your natural curiosity? But it is done, and thankfully without harm to either of you."

He turned to Jack. "Perhaps there is little purpose in explaining why we have sought you."The tinner inclined his head, and Corantyn went on."Then you will lend your aid?"

"It seems I have already begun," came the answer. "The matter is too serious for me to sit idly by. There is much to do, and for my part, I will delay no longer. For now, Corantyn, do you and Gawen escort this wayward pair to their home; the day is drawing to an end. They have lost their ponies but never fear," he smiled warmly at them,"I will find them. The seeking may lead me to discover more of Pengersek's plans."

"Take care, tinner," warned Gawen."It would not do for the Witch-Lord to discover that you walk these hills."

"Why's that?" said John inquisitively.

The tinner replied enigmatically, "Our paths have crossed before."

THE sun was dipping to the western horizon as the weary children, guided along ancient paths by Corantyn and Gawen, passed the high ramparts of the prehistoric fort of Caer Brân. The hill on which it stood commanded a wide view over the southern plain of West Penwith, covered in a patchwork of fields, and deeply incised by the Penberth valley and the wooded vales that wound down to Lamorna Cove. To the south, the tower of St Buryan seemed a long way off.

"How long will it take us to get home?" asked Penny wearily as they made their way down the hill towards the first of the farm fields. Her feet hurt and it seemed as though they'd been walking for hours.

"By the paths known to us," Corantyn replied, "little more than an hour."

John was feeling downright miserable. "I don't fancy having to do the explaining," he muttered "Ben'll have a fit when he finds out we've lost the . . . Oooofff!"

A violent shove in the back pitched him, sprawling, into a heap among the gorse bushes.

11: FOGOU

"WHAT'S the game?" hissed John angrily. "What did you shove me like that for?"

Corantyn pressed a hand to the boy's lips and cautiously raised his head to peer over the gorse. "There!" he whispered urgently, pointing his finger towards the brow of the hill. John crept forward to look.

On the northern skyline, a shade-like figure stood beside his horse, one hand raised to shield his eyes from the rays of the setting sun.

"There!" said Gawen quietly, pointing further to the left. "And there. All seven have come."

The horsemen were spaced out along the skyline, from a point close to Caer Brân to another halfway up the slope of Bartinney Hill. All were as Penny had seen them before; darkly cloaked and hooded, and they stood like statues as they scanned the landscape for their prey.

"It's them!" Penny felt fear deep in the pit of her stomach.

John understood immediately. "But I thought they only came out at night. The sun hasn't set yet."

"They can emerge from the mists an hour before sun-set," Corantyn explained, "and can remain at large until an hour before sunrise. Though they seldom need to sport for that long," he added grimly.

Gawen glanced at the growing yellows of the western sky, and at the blood-red ball of the sun balancing on the sea horizon. "Come," he said, "the light may yet be too strong for their eyes. I would rather be putting distance between us, than skulk behind this flimsy bush."

He moved away to lead them, crouching and rolling, through the undergrowth, and they gritted their teeth against the painful jabs of the gorse spines which lay thickly on the ground. An overgrown stone hedge appeared in front of them and they found a gate to wriggle under before pausing in the shelter of the hedge, safe from searching eyes; a place to catch their breath and to think.

"D'you think they saw us?" panted John anxiously.

As if in reply, the shrill cry of a horn reached their ears; a sound to chill the very marrow of their bones.

"We are undone!" exclaimed Corantyn. "They stand between us and our onlysanctuaries. See: they waited for us to pass by the fort of Caer Brân and the old earthwork of Bartinnê, for these are places they cannot enter. John and Penny, you have not our speed and stamina. I have an idea; before us is an old droveway which passes close to the settlement of Carn Euny. In these days it is an ancient curiosity, but it contains what was once a sacred place. It may still be so. I have no suggestion other than that you must take refuge there while Gawen and I try to lead the hunters away. It is the only course left open to us."

"But what if they catch you?" Penny protested.

"We must see that they do not. They may not seek to slay us . . . they are not in quest of wandering elf nor warrior dwarf, only of those they will find in our company. On the other hand, we cannot be certain."

Corantyn led the way as they scuttled down the wide grassy track. finally coming to a halt behind the corner of a tall hedge. Following his pointing finger, they saw a stile and beyond it, a wooden hut.

"The village of Carn Euny lies there," said the elf. "That is the custodian's hut, but at this time of the evening he will be at his home. Beyond the hut lie the remains of a village built some two thousand years ago, and hidden among its walls you will find a fogou. Conceal yourselves there and await our return."

"A what-did-you-call-it?" said John.

"A fogou; an underground passage which was the sacred shrine of those who lived here. It is a useful refuge and if any of its ancient sanctity remains, it may keep the Nôshelyas at bay. Only within the fogou itself will such protection be effective, therefore be sure to remain inside. Quickly now, there is no time to lose. May the Mother protect you – and us."

"Be careful -" Penny began, but John seized her arm as he turned to race for the ancient village. They kept close to the hedge, stooping low to avoid detection. Behind them, Corantyn and Gawen hurried away, down the hill and out of sight.

Carn Euny was an Iron Age settlement, and the stunted walls of the circular stone houses provided plentiful cover as they searched for the mysterious fogou.

"Look here!" whispered John. "This must be it."

At their feet was a path which sloped into the ground, and the dark, square portal of the ancient passage. The fogou was a long, curving gallery, with inward leaning walls of the dry stone masonry typical of its Celtic builders. Its roof was of great slabs laid crossways, and the passage was more than six feet in both height and width. By its northern entrance was a small opening to a short passage which led into an astonishing bell-shaped chamber built completely below ground. The top of its roof was missing, leaving the chamber open to the sky.

Near the southern end of the main gallery was a tiny entrance leading into another side passage only big enough to admit a man on his hands and knees. Angling steeply up to the surface, it had been dubbed by archaeologists a creep. The entire structure was wonderfully preserved and it hardly seemed possible that it was so old. Whether or not its ancient holiness, the spirit of the Earth Mother, remained, the fogou contained a feeling of deep peace which seemed to embrace and comfort them.

John was suitably impressed. "Well," he said, "this is handy. Even if we're found, there's more than one way out." He pointed at the little entrance to the creep passage. "I won't be seen if I wriggle up there and have a look. I must see if Corantyn and Gawen are all right."

"Be careful!" Penny whispered as he crawled into the little passage.

Where the creep opened to the air, a low bank concealed him from hostile eyes but gave him a good view to the south as he cautiously peered out. In the deepening gloom it took him a moment to spot the two fleeing figures making speed across the fields, hurling themselves over gates and hedges. The dwarf could move at an astonishing rate for one so small, and he matched the long legs of Corantyn stride for stride.

The twilight was filled with shouts and a rider galloped loudly down the track they had left only moments earlier. He reined in sharply near the entrance to the prehistoric village, jabbing a gloved finger in the direction that Gawen and Corantyn had taken. He twisted in his saddle, raising a curved horn to his hidden lips, and another of the terrible hunting calls rang out.

It was then that John spotted a sleek form slinking to the huntsman's side. A second joined it, and the boy noted the loping gait on silent pads, the alert ears and gleaming eyes. He drew a sharp breath, for despite the impossibility, he knew they were wolves, and the fear of them gnawed at his stomach. He ducked smartly back into the darkness of the fogou, his heart pounding at his ribs.

John and Penny crouched in the silent gloom for what seemed an age, scarcely daring to breathe. For some time they could hear the drumming of hoofs and the chill voice of the horn until, at last, an uneasy quiet descended, broken only by the barking of foxes somewhere on the hill.

"I think they've gone." Penny's whisper could scarcely be heard.

"I hope they have," said John. "Stay here. I'll have a look."

Penny sat alone in the gloom, waiting. There was a sound, somewhere in the darkness.

"John?" Her voice was small, frightened. It was an awful snuffling sound. She turned and saw a black, hunched shape

She heard the low, throaty growl

blocking the far exit. Golden eyes glittered and she heard a low, throaty growl.

For a moment, Penny stood transfixed but, as the creature growled again, she began to back away. It started forward, into the entrance of the fogou, but stopped abruptly as if it had run into an impenetrable barrier. Confused, it stood still, its eyes glaring down the length of the passage. Suddenly it began a frenzied attack, snapping and snarling, on the invisible force which prevented its entry.

Penny's fright drove her backwards, away from its vicious fury. Then she felt the cool breeze on her cheek and realised, to her horror, that her retreat had brought her through the exit and outside the protection of the fogou.

The icy, vice-like grasp of the hand which clamped onto her shoulder brought a terrible scream to her throat.

John was not to hear any of this. Having reached the top of the creep, he pushed his head stealthily out into the open. At first, he could see nothing, then, as he turned his head, his mouth fell open and a yelp of fright died in his throat.

Six inches from his eyes was a booted foot and the hem of a robe, the colour of night. The silent figure stooped over him. The boy stared up into the black maw of the hood, and what little remained of his courage melted away. Twin points of pale light, seemingly floating in emptiness, glared down from the reeking darkness beneath the cowl.

Then, he felt a hard blow high to the side of his head, and the world, the night, and its terrors, fell away.

IT was dark in the little grey town of St Just. The only light came from the moon, almost full, which danced in and out of small, fleecy clouds. Folk slept soundly but a brindled dog, wandering near the church, raised its hackles, whimpered softly, and slunk away.

The hoofs of an unseen horse clattered on the roadway and a voice, soft and made of shadows, called gently into the night: " Selus . . . Selus, noble duke, brother of holy Justin, son of Gerent the Brave. Now is the time to leave thy stone. The Darkness rises before us. Awake and come forth, O holy warrior."

A wind sprang from nowhere, rushed past and was gone. The church door creaked softly and, from the darkness of the porch, a man stepped forth. He was tall, and his bearing noble. Moonlight played on his breastplate and on the hilt of his sword. Dark hair rested on his shoulders and there was light in the watchful eyes.

He paused briefly on the path among the gravestones. The horse snorted impatiently until, with a swirl of his cloak, the figure turned and strode swiftly from the churchyard. The hoofs rang again on the tarmac, then, with the rising of a strong breeze from the west, they could be heard as they galloped away, down the steep path to the valley below. Somewhere in the night a dog barked briefly and fell silent.

Within the dark sanctity of the church, an old stone stood among the pews. The moonlight, filtering a myriad of colours through the stained glass windows, illuminated the faint ChiRho carving on its face,and picked out the words carved in its side fifteen centuries before: SELVS IC IACIT

IT was deep into the night when Penny woke to find herself lying on a lonely hill-side, her body cushioned by thick heather.

A man, leading a horse, was walking slowly towards her from a long, low ruin of tumbled and overgrown stone. The light of the moon shone full upon his face and she knew him. Having cast off the unkempt, eccentric guise of Henry Milliton, Marek, Lord of Pengersek, was perhaps the most handsome man she had ever seen.

Tall and powerful, he wore a flowing mantle of rich, dark cloth, edged with crimson and open at the front to reveal black robes of finest eastern silk beneath. Around the flowing waves of his dark hair was a metal band, set with the seven jewels of the seven planets, and about his waist was a wide girdle of leather, inscribed in gold with mystic symbols. Bearded, keen-eyed and noble, the Lord of Pengersek smiled on her with gentleness and mercy.

Doubt flooded into her confused, frightened mind. Surely this man could not be the Satanic sorcerer, the Witch-Lord of whom she had been told? Then she saw the sorcerer's familiar, the coal-black demon mare whose breath steamed like brimstone in the night air and whose eyes, glaring balefully at her, burned with a hellish light. And the eyes of the sorcerer himself were not gazing so benevolently at her, but at the Crownstone which hung from her neck.

Her hand flew to the stone, grasping it tightly. "No!" she gasped. "You shan't have it!" She tried to move, to get up and run, but the strength had been drawn from her and she lay helpless.

Still she gripped the stone, and its cold facets seemed to strengthen her courage. "You shan't touch it. Never!" Her jaw was set and her eyes fixed on Pengersek's defiantly.

The sorcerer's expression of compassion did not change. Instead, he stretched out a hand and spoke softly. "My child . . . my poor, frightened child. You have suffered so much terror. Come, my fireside shall banish the chill of the night and my harp strings shall bring peace to your troubled mind."

It was then she saw that he carried a small harp which he nestled into his shoulder. Long fingers gently played across the strings and the exquisite chords floated in rings and spirals around her. Pengersek's voice joined the beautiful sounds and it was soft and fine, the voice of an accomplished bard. The words were in a language she knew to be Cornish. She would never know if she truly understood them, but her mind flooded with visions of turquoise waters and playing dolphins, soft sands and a gentle sun. The magic of the music worked its spell and, try as she might, gritting her teeth and covering her ears, she could not resist its subtle effect. She found herself slipping back into oblivion.

And yet before the velvet darkness closed around her, it seemed as though the ruin behind the sorcerer was changing its shape: shimmering and shivering upwards into proud, grey, impregnable walls.

JOHN opened his eyes. The bright light of morning lanced into them and he shut them quickly. He tried a second time, pain drumming inside his head. He gingerly felt the spot where he had been struck. There was a large bump and blood had matted his hair, and run down the side of his face. He lay on the floor of the fogou's main passage, having apparently tumbled down the creep. The light of a new day streamed through the entrance to the tunnel, and he shivered. Groggily he clambered to his feet, seeking the support of the walls. A nauseating giddiness swept through him but, gritting his teeth and rocking unsteadily on his feet, he looked up and down the passage, and realised that he was alone.

He called out for Penny, but no answer came. He peered into the empty creep, then tottered along the passage to the round side chamber. That, too, was empty and quiet.

Close to panic, John staggered out into the sunlight, clutching his head.

"Oy!" yelled a voice. The boy winced painfully as the shout stabbed into his aching head. "Wot the 'ell are you doin' 'ere?"

It was the custodian of the ancient monument, a burly figure, bustling officiously out of his hut. "Well, got a tongue, 'ave 'ee? You 'abm paid . . . 'Ere, that's a nasty bang! 'It yer 'ead down the fogou, did 'ee?"

John nodded. It hurt and he was still unsteady on his feet.

"You oughta get that seen to. 'Ow long 'ave 'ee been 'ere?"

"All night, I think."

"All night! Damme, boy, yer folks'll be worried sick!"

"Not as much as they will be when they find out I've lost Penny."

"Penny? Who's that?"

"My sister. And Corantyn . . . why hasn't he come back?" His mind whirled frantically.

"An' who would that be?"

"A friend. An elf."

The custodian boggled at him. "If you said what I think you said, then I d'reckon that knock on the noddle's done more damage than I thought! I edn got no phone 'ere; edn got no first aid kit, neither. The number o' times I been on to the Commission 'bout that. Best thing you can do is make yer way down to the farm. Just down there, tes. No distance 'tall. I can't go leavin' my post; tes more'n me job's worth – "

"Thanks," said John, drily. "I'll be okay."

"Elves!" repeated the custodian.

John walked away. The trip-hammer behind his eyes was beating a little more gently now, and his only thought was to get back to Trehelya Vean. He'd have to explain it all to Ben; Ben would know what to do. He looked around. Yes, those cottages, half a mile or so across the fields, must be Crows-an-wra, and a lane led from there to St Buryan.

He set off across the fields, walking at first, then breaking into a run as he passed the hump of a prehistoric tomb and crossed a stream. Thoughts as to what might have happened to Penny spurred him on; none of them were exactly pleasant.

He heard a rumble, looked up, and saw the windows of a coach packed with sight-seers on an early morning trip to Land's End. The road! Only another field away! He drove himself on and the effort made his head spin. Oh no! he thought, not now! Please, not now!

Over the hedge he scrambled, and onto the grass verge. He stood there, panting for breath. Again his head swam, and through the roaring in his ears, there came a familiar sound. He felt dizzy and wanted to be sick, but, with a last, despairing effort, he raised his drooping head to see the glorious sight of a blue Land Rover turning out of the St Buryan lane.

"Ben!" he croaked, and toppled, senseless, to the ground.

12: WITCH HUNT

FAR away a voice was raised in anger; slowly it grew louder and nearer. John was convinced that the words were directed at himself and he struggled to understand them. He tried weakly to answer, his mind forming the phrases 'It was my fault . . . all my fault . . . I'm sorry . . . I tried . . . I tried . . .'but they left his lips only as a wordless groan. The angry voice halted in mid-flow and a shadow fell across his mist-filled eyes.

"John?" It was the same voice, Ben's voice, softer now, but urgent and anxious. "Easy now, boy. You're home. You're safe."

"Ben?" John wiped a hand across his eyes to clear them and to rid himself of the painful thumping in his head. His vision swam slowly into focus. Around him were the friendly, warm surroundings of Trehelya Vean. He was lying on the settee, his uncle's craggy face peering down at him.

"How do 'ee feel?" Ben asked softly.

"I'm not sure. My head aches like mad, but I think I'm all right."

The farmer smiled grimly. "Must have a skull like a coconut. You've taken a hell of a crack. How do 'ee feel 'bout sittin' up?"

John eased himself into a more upright position, blinking painfully. He glanced about the room, and all but fell off the settee in his surprise. Corantyn and Gawen were there, seated somewhat uncomfortably at the table, at the head of which sat Ned Hosken. The farmhand held a shotgun that was pointing at a spot directly between the strange pair, and the double barrel was as steady as a rock. In a corner behind him lay Gawen's war-axe, and Corantyn's bow, quiver and dagger. Nellie Hosken was also there, perched nervously on the edge of a chair, white-faced and awe-struck. Her eyes were goggling at the elf and dwarf.

Ben sat on the arm of the settee, laying a protective arm on John's shoulders. "Now that the lad's come round," he said menacingly, "we'll have your story again an' God help 'ee if there's so much as a word of a lie. John'll tell me the truth of'n, and judgin' by what's been said already, I wouldn't be in your shoes. Now, let's hear it."

It was Corantyn who elected to speak, and he related the story of the sorcerer Pengersek and his lust for the power of the Crownstone; of how John and Penny had unwittingly released the mysterious forces of Boscawen-ûn which, in turn, had woken all manner of strangeness; of Penny's flight and escape from the Night Hunters; everything up to their final peril at Carn Euny.

Ben listened impatiently but quietly. "Well, boy?" he said finally. "Tes the same tale he gave me earlier. Now, what's the truth of 'n?"

"I know it sounds fantastic," John looked earnestly at his uncle, "but it's all true. Every word of it. Corantyn and Gawen are friends . . . they've done everything they can to help us. They even tried to draw the Hunters away from us last night, but they had wolves to sniff us out. They took Penny and laid me out."

"Wolves?" Ben gasped. "But there hab'm been wolves in this country for centuries! No, John, they must've been dogs; Alsatians, p'raps."

"No," said Corantyn, flatly. "They were wolves; called from the Shadowlands to serve the Nôshelyas." Ben gaped at him.

"But how did you manage to get away?" John asked Corantyn.

"We ran for all we were worth, hoping to gain Treryn Dinas, but they were too fast and intent in their purpose. Six followed us; one remained. I knew then that all of us were lost. Death was

in the wind, but our one hope of remaining alive was to seek
shelter here. There is no mercy in the Nôshelyas, and yet" – the
dark, blank eyes narrowed in thought – "they let you live. This
I do not understand."

"He is a Trevelyan," Gawen broke in. "There is the reason.
As the Trevelyans are the rightful owners of the Crownstone, so
do they all come within its powers of protection. Thus, the
Nôshelyas were powerless to slay him and since we, too, live,
they were also powerless to storm the house of a Trevelyan."

Ben snorted derisively. "Protection? What protection?
They've laid the lad's head open, dammit; and God only knows
what they've done with Penny. Where the hell's the protection in
that?"

"Are they not alive? By the same token that John has
survived, Penny will not be harmed," said the dwarf, bluntly.

Ben stared coldly at him for a long moment, then turned back
to John. "Tes the doctor for you, boy," he said. "Nellie's done a
proper job of washin' an' dressin' the wound, but tes always best
to be safe."

"Let me see it." Corantyn got up from his chair, ignoring the
threatening wave of the gun barrel. Ben stood aside, wary of the
strange being and his fathomless eyes. The elf gently unwrapped
the bandage and studied the injury. "No doctor will be necessary," he said. "The blood has made it look worse than it is; the
cut is small and not deep. Better still, there is no concussion or
ill-effect. I can heal this wound and remove the pain, but you,
farmer Trevelyan, must allow me to go out and gather the herbs
I will need."

Ben hesitated. "Go on, then," he decided. "But be quick
about it. An' don't even think about pullin' a fast one, 'cause
your mate is stayin' right here. Understood?"

Corantyn made no reply, but strode quickly to the door and
went out.

"Ben, you must trust them," John pleaded. "They really are
on our side. They risked their lives for us last night."

The farmer let out a long sigh. "I knaw, boy, but see it from
my point o' view. There's an almighty 'ammerin' on the door in
the middle of the night, and when I open it, there's these two,

lookin' like somethin' out o' the Brothers Grimm. The little fella's wavin' an axe that could cut a man in 'alf, an' as for the other one, I damn near passed out when I clapped eyes on him!

"You talk to me 'bout trust, John. You need to see into someone's eyes to even start trustin' em; but you can't see a thing in his – if you've even got the nerve to look at 'em in the first place."

Corantyn returned quickly with his handful of herbs and asked for a bowl in which to prepare them. Nellie ushered him dumbly into the kitchen. Moments later he returned with a thin, almost colourless paste. The elf's hands moved expertly around the injury applying the mixture.

John blinked. A curious wave seemed to pass over him and he put a hesitant hand to his head. "What did you do?" he exclaimed, "the pain's gone!"

Corantyn gave him a half-smile. "It is an old secret," he replied. "Another you Men have lost. One day, perhaps, I may teach it to you. In an hour, maybe less, there will be little trace of any hurt."

Ben looked momentarily relieved, but set his jaw as he thought of his niece's plight. "How do we get Penny back from Milliton, or whatever you say his real name is? I don't see much point in draggin' the police in; they'd never believe a single word o' this. We'd be the ones being locked up!"

He began to pace about the room. "By God!" he cried suddenly, "if that misfit's so much as harmed one hair of her head – !"

"There you can rest assured," said Corantyn calmly. "He will not have harmed her, for he cannot. He knows full well that the Crownstone would destroy him in an instant. But she will be ensorcelled, of that I am certain."

"What does that mean?" Ben demanded.

"She will be asleep, and know nothing of what is happening. Pengersek can do this by harp-magic alone. It is a powerful spell, but harmless. As for the Crownstone: only by sorcery can he achieve anything with it, and it will be night-magic, long in the making. The Nôshelyas encircled this farm well into the early hours of this morning, then left as though called away. Their captain must have come, and Penny with him, and they would have returned to the Witch-Lord together, for they do not like to be separated for long. There was not enough of the night left for Pengersek to perform the spells necessary to wrest the power from the Crownstone and bend it to his will."

"Now just wait a moment!" Ben broke in, "this is something I can do myself, without your help or anyone else's. God knaws why I didn't think o' this earlier. I knaw where Milliton lives: tedn no more'n a ten minute drive. That settles it. I'm goin' over there right now. I'll sort that lunatic out an' make a proper job of 'n. Should 've been done months ago!"

John was aghast. "But, Ben! It's not that simple. He's got fantastic powers - You wouldn't stand an earthly against him!"

"That is so," said Corantyn. "Pengersek, the man you call Henry Milliton, could easily strike you down at will. His ancient mastery of the Black Arts – "

"Won't save him from a good hiding!" Ben cut in sharply. "I'll be damned if I let myself be put off that easily. No, my friend, Milliton's goin' to wish he'd never heard of St Buryan an' the Trevelyans! Ned, keep an eye on 'em till I get back." The door slammed shut behind him, and they listened helplessly as the Land Rover shot furiously out of the farmyard.

John was beside himself. "Why wouldn't he listen!" he cried.

"He is angered and worried," said Corantyn. "There is no room in that for reason. Do not fret; he will come to no harm. Pengersek will not be there."

"What?" John gaped at him. "Then where is he? How will we find him?"

"Would that I knew." The elf sat down beside Gawen again, paying little heed to Ned Hosken and his shotgun. "However, my belief is that he is still in Belerion: a small land, true, but with so many hidden places. We will need time – "

"Which we do not have," said a laconic voice from the doorway. They looked up sharply – in the case of Ned and his wife, with alarm – to see the bizarre figure of Jack of the Hammer leaning casually against the door-jamb. "But," he added, "there may yet be a way. Do you so easily forget the holed stone of Gûnajynyal?"

Gawen's face broke into a beam of delight. "The tinner is right! The holed stone!" The smile faded. "But does it still have its powers? It has suffered much abuse."

"You, old cleaver, would doubt the sunrise if it was blinding your eyes," said Jack mischievously. "It would take more than the mere meddlings of men to rob that stone of its properties."

"Then we must leave at once!" exclaimed Corantyn sharply.

"We certainly should," Jack agreed. "To that end, I have brought horses, including those you so carelessly lost yesterday on the moor, young Trevelyan."

"Now just 'ang on a minute," growled Ned. "I dunnaw who you are, mister, but no one's goin' anywhere till Ben gets back."

"But Ned!" John pleaded, "we haven't got any choice!"

"Time," said the tinner, ambling into the room, "is the one thing which cannot be spared. It strikes me that such a complex and powerful rite as that which Pengersek must perform can only succeed on one of four nights of the year, and then only if the moon is full. This coming night is one of those four – the Eve of Golowan – and the moon is full.

"We have until midnight only, little more than sixteen hours by my reckoning, to find the girl and the stone, and free them. Midnight, my friends; a minute beyond will be too late."

"An' if 'ee don't find her by then?" Ned demanded.

The tinner's affable expression faded. "It is best you do not ask."

John looked up wildly. "Ned, please! You've got to let us go!"

Alarm showed on the old farm-hand's face, uncertain of the course he should take. Jack of the Hammer walked slowly over to him and turned the gun barrel away. Ned's shoulders slumped and he looked down at the floor, defeated.

"Twadn loaded, anyhow," he muttered.

Jack's hand rested lightly on the old man's shoulder. "You are a good man, Ned Hosken, and loyal to your old friend. But in this we are right, believe me. We must leave without delay, but when the farmer returns, tell him that he may find us at the Mên-an-tol."

BEN switched the engine off and studied Milliton's cottage through the windscreen. It was a gaunt, granite builing which had seen better times, and stood in isolation a mile or so from St Buryan. The roof was in poor repair, with any number of slates dislodged or missing altogether: one or two had slid down the roof and caught in the moss-clogged gutter. The cracked, filthy windows stared blankly back at him.

Ben recalled a night, some weeks earlier, when he'd been walking along this lane. On approaching the cottage he'd heard eerie sounds from within, and seen ghostly lights flickering through holes and chinks in the moth-eaten curtain. The place had seemed to attract a cloud of darkness and he had heard Milliton's voice, raised in a strange and monotonous chant. The farmer remembered how his skin had crept, how there'd seemed to be a reaching hand of fear, and how he'd quickened his steps towards the village and the friendly lights of the St Buryan Inn.

He also recalled the evening following the incident involving the vicar and Milliton's horse, which had been the main topic in the pub that night. Everyone seemed to agree that Milliton was a misfit, maybe even a dangerous one, but, like an unspoken thread running through the conversation, there was an undercurrent of thought – which most villagers kept to themselves – that there was a certain something about Milliton that they'd rather not discuss. Strangely, it had been the vicar who'd come the closest to touching on this.

"For all his pleasantries," he'd remarked, "I sense that the man is no Christian; indeed he's said as much himself. As for that brute of a horse, it's like no other horse I've ever come across. It's a menace to the public. Perhaps I shouldn't say this but, to me, the man radiates evil. Have any of you noticed that pendant he wears? Do you know what it is – what it represents? No? – It's the inverted pentacle; one of the signs used by those who practise the Black Arts!"

Ben stalked past the garden gate which lay drunkenly to one side. The front door of the cottage was shut and, like the gate, its paintwork had peeled off in great flakes that littered the doorstep. Dank moss coated its foot.

He stood back from the door and smashed the sole of his boot against it with all the force of his pent-up anger. It flew inwards, hinges tearing from the rotten jambs.

Dust lay everywhere in deep layers, and the pit of the farmer's stomach turned cold as he realised that it was the collection of ages. Not a single footprint had disturbed it. No one had set foot in the cottage for years and yet this was Milliton's house. He had seen the man come and go with his own eyes. It made no sense.

Ben decided to take a look at the upstairs room in which he had seen those lights and heard that chanting voice. Almost at once he knew it was pointless when the bottom step of the narrow staircase disintegrated under the weight of his foot. Confused and bewildered, he retreated into the hallway and stood for a while to collect his thoughts.

He shivered. A deep chill had soaked into the air around him and it seemed that even the sunlight outside had slunk away. Shadows were forming where none had been before, and the farmer began to sense the presence of a nameless evil. His eyes darted to the dark stairway and the breath hissed through his teeth.

In the gloom, something was beginning to take shape, and the specks of dust which hung in the air were sucked towards it. Hanging in mid-air was a face, long and dark, with a hint of baleful eyes which burned with a fiery light. Great nostrils flared redly and the foaming mouth champed on an unseen bit. Hoofs clattered loudly on the bare floorboards and Ben clapped his hands to his ears as the apparition bellowed an ear-shattering whinny of rage. He flinched away, and the instinctive movement saved him as an iron-clad hoof ripped through the air where his head had been and smashed into the wall, tearing a gaping hole in the crumbling lath and plaster.

The farmer staggered backwards. His heels caught the edge of the fallen door and he pitched over, rolling helplessly back through the doorway and out onto the garden path.

The spell was broken. A shrill neigh of fury was cut off in mid-cry as Ben, on his knees, stared back into the gloomy house. But the thing had vanished. He was in no doubt as to what he had just seen. It was Milliton's mare; the sorcerer's familiar.

A derisive remark made earlier that day by Gawen came to his mind: "Mare? Ha! A demon! A demon in horse-shape!"

Ben turned from the cottage and unashamedly ran.

Once in the Land Rover, he sat resting his head on the steering wheel. His breath came in whooping gasps; his heart pounded against his ribs and he found himself trembling from head to foot.

After a few moments he glanced up, frowning. Something was wrong . . . different. Yes, that was it, the shadows weren't in the right place. He'd parked against a hedge which had been full in the light of the sun. Now, it was in shadow. It was impossible; the sun could not have marched halfway across the sky in just a few minutes.

Almost in panic, he looked at his watch and shook his head again and again, unable to believe what it confirmed. Since entering the cottage, surely no more than five minutes before, more than four hours had passed.

PART TWO

SHALL TIMES INTERMINGLE?

13: ORACLE AND IRONSTONE

A STIFFENING breeze keened over the desolate moor, whipping John's hair back from his eyes as he gazed at the curious stones among the furze. There were three of them, all about four feet high and set in a straight line. The two end stones were stubby menhirs but it was the central one that captured his attention. This was a wheel-shaped slab, standing on its rim and pierced by a perfectly round hole just big enough for a grown man to crawl through. The Mên-an-tol had stood on the moor called Gûnajynyal since time out of mind and none could now tell why, when or by whose hand it had been set up.

According to Jack, it possessed peculiar properties which country folk, and even those who considered themselves more 'civilised', still sought out, although few ever owned to doing so. The stone was a healer. All manner of back ailments were supposed to be cured simply by performing the ritual of crawling round the stone in the opposite direction to the path of the sun, squeezing through the hole on each of the nine prescribed circuits. It was said that it was at its most potent on Midsummer Eve, the Eve of Golowan, and that the patient should observe the ritual unclothed.

"Should you be here tonight," Jack told him, "you would laugh to see the fun. People from all walks of life, the rich and the poor, creeping through the hole as naked and pink as the day they were born. I cannot say whether or not they receive any true healing from the stone; I have never had cause to try it."

"Then why are we here?" said John. "I don't see that being cured of backache is going to get us any nearer to finding Penny."

"And yet I have hope that it will find her," Jack replied. "You see, the Mên-an-tol is also an oracle. It has been known to answer certain questions, if it is willing."

"It used to," said Gawen, "but will it now? The stones have suffered much; they have been moved around more than once that I know."

Jack nodded. "They have indeed been moved, but it is beyond the powers of men to remove such properties from the stones. We shall see."

"You are well versed in lore such as this, master tinner," said Corantyn. "Will the stone answer to you?"

"I can only try."

"But the pins," pressed the elf. "For this, two pins must be used, and they must be fashioned of brass. Such things are rare these days."

For answer, Jack unslung his tool-bag, rummaged around inside it, smiled and triumphantly held up a pair of long, gleaming pins. They were brass. Gawen laughed. "My question," he chuckled, "is what do you not keep in there?"

Jack grinned at him, then placed the pins crosswise on top of the holed stone. He drew the hammer from his belt and laid it down beside the leather bag. Kneeling before the stone, he placed both hands flat against its sides, his forehead lightly touching its cold surface.

For some moments he remained there, silent and unmoving, his thoughts reaching out for the mysterious power of the Mên-an-tol. At last, he spoke. The words were soft, barely audible, but as John listened, he felt more than ever that there was much to this strange man that he did not know.

"Stone of healing and guidance, tell me the wish of my heart. I seek the daughter of Trevelyan who bears the Crownstone of Lyonesse, lately returned from the deep; and the Witch-Lord,

Jack placed the pins crosswise on top of the holed stone

Marek of Pengersek, into whose hands she has fallen. Evil befalls the land of Belerion, and the Eve of Golowan is upon us. Hear now my plea, silent oracle; show me what I truly seek."

John had no idea what to expect. The ageless stone remained silent.

"The pins," Gawen whispered. "See, they move!"

One of the pins was indeed moving; at first, an almost imperceptible motion, then, jerking slightly as though it were steel and reacting to the pull of a magnet, the other began to stir. The tinner's face was lined and strained as he fought to meld his mind to the power of the holed stone and keep it there; the invisible forces flowed back and forth between rock and man.

Slowly the pins uncrossed until they had formed the shape of a V, then all movement ceased. The pulsing current rested once more within the crystals of the rock. Jack rested where he knelt for a moment or two before climbing unsteadily to his feet. His face was pale and drawn as though his energy had been sucked from him.

"I had forgotten that the holed stone is apt to sap the strength from the bones," he wheezed. "I am told that it is a brief effect – let us hope that it is. So, let us see if the stone has seen fit to answer."

He turned his eyes to the pointer formed by the pins and raised his head to follow the indicated direction. His face hardened. The smiling face John had come to know became white with suppressed rage, and the eyes, merry no longer, were points of flint. The tinner's hands balled into tight, white-knuckled fists, and his breath hissed angrily through clenched teeth. Then, just as quickly, he relaxed and his features re-assumed their more familiar expression.

"So! There is the sorcerer's lair." He pointed. "It makes our task none the easier." A mile and a half to the south-west there rose a round hill and the dark, broken line of ruined walls lay upon its summit.

"Chûn Castle," said Corantyn quietly. Gawen pursed his bearded lips and said nothing. Again, John glimpsed silent fury on the tinner's face. "We have only till midnight," the elf continued, "and this is the Eve of Golowan."

"I don't understand you!" John burst out. "Any of you! What's so difficult about it? I've seen the place; it's nothing but a ruin. The walls are all broken down – you can walk in over them!"

"I cannot deny that it is as you say," said Corantyn. "But believe this, John. Should you approach in anger, you would find those same walls restored to their full height and splendour. Such is the sorcery of the Witch-Lord, and that is what we are pitted against: sorcery. Remember, none of us is a magician."

Jack retrieved the pins and returned them to his tool-bag. "We need two things above all else," he said, "and quickly. Further aid, and a plan of action that may work. A tall order."

John felt uneasy as they walked away from the Mên-an-tol. For some little time he had been aware of a tingling at the nape of his neck as though hidden eyes were watching. He hung back a little, his own eyes darting furtively from side to side. Corantyn saw his hesitancy and walked back to his side. The elf's head was held at a slight angle, all senses alert. Jack and Gawen, deep in conversation and unaware of their companions' unease, carried on ahead towards the rough lane where their horses waited.

"Your senses do not deceive you," Corantyn murmured to the boy. "We have been watched since we came to the holed stone. I have been vigilant, but have seen nothing. The spy is well concealed, whoever he is."

John wondered whether they ought to alert Jack and Gawen, but they were too far ahead. A gorse bush rattled behind them and from the corner of his eye, John glimpsed a dim shape leaping out onto the path. The boy whirled and froze, his face reflecting the horror of the thing that faced him.

It was not far short of man height, but seemed smaller as it hunched, ready to spring. The body of the creature, clad in nothing more than a ragged hide, and the disproportionately long limbs, were terribly wasted and thin, belying their wiry strength. The skin was pale, with a greyish tinge, and the clawed hands and feet were large and splayed. Puny shoulders and a scrawny, corded neck supported a massive head, domed and hairless, with bluish, knotted veins which bulged grotesquely. The slitted eyes were yellow, and a great hook of a nose jutted over the shapeless gash of a mouth which stretched back almost as far as the high, pointed ears. Sharp teeth bared in a snarl of animal hatred.

Ancient instinct drove the thing. The high-arching nostrils had smelt elf; its traditional and most hated enemy since the dawn of time. It was well aware that it stood one against two, but its primitive senses told it that one was petrified with fear. Maybe it could kill swiftly and be gone before the others could react.

It paused for a split second, then sprang murderously at Corantyn. A greenstone dagger flashed in the claw-like hand, but the elf was lightning-quick, moving forward and ducking smartly under the downward swing of the knife. He crashed into the wasted body and both fell heavily. The creature rolled away and up onto its feet with the speed of a cat. Corantyn was up almost as fast, but his heel snagged awkwardly in his own bowstring and he stumbled to his knees. The creature pounced, its bony heels landing hard on Corantyn's back, forcing the elf flat, and it snarled horribly with triumph as it raised the knife for the kill.

A small, dark object whizzed past John's ear and struck the grotesque being full in the chest. There was a short, thin scream, a brilliant flash of flame, and the loathsome thing seemed to crumple into itself. An acrid stench stung the boy's nostrils and then there was nothing but grey ash which settled into a small heap on the grass.

Pale-faced, Corantyn got to his feet as Jack strode past him to retrieve his ironstone charm. He shook it free of ash and hung it once more about his neck.

John stared open-mouthed at the pile of ash. "What was it?" he said, thickly.

"No friend of ours," said Jack. "You know now what a spriggan looks like, and things are taking a grave turn if they are now daring to skulk under the eye of the sun without their mists and squalls to hide them. How is it with you, Corantyn?"

"I am unhurt," answered the elf. "My thanks, tinner. The ironstone is bane indeed to these goblins."

"One at a time, perhaps," remarked Jack, eyeing the ash

which was now beginning to scatter before the breeze. "It will not be so useful if we have to face a horde of his kindred."

Things had taken a terrible turn and John felt sick to his stomach. For the first time, death had entered the scene and its awful presence roused the thought which, above all else, had been gnawing at his mind. He set his jaw as the question he'd not yet dared to voice found its way into words. "Please – I want the truth. I've heard about these Black Magic ceremonies and things. They sacrifice people, don't they?"

Jack placed a kindly hand on his shoulder. "There are cases where they do, John, but not, I believe, in this one. I have two reasons for saying this: first, Pengersek seeks to become greater in power than any other, therefore he sees no one to whom he will offer a sacrifice. Secondly, he dare not harm your sister, nor touch the Crownstone itself for fear of his own destruction. He will no doubt have treated her with every gentleness. He has no other choice, and only high sorcery at the appointed hour can touch the Stone." His grip became firmer and John looked into eyes that held only sincerity.

"You ask me for truth, John, and I will give you truth, hiding nothing and sparing nothing. There is a real and fearful danger for Penny, and it is this. Should Pengersek succeed in wresting the power from the Crownstone, the force of his spell, combined with the sudden and terrible release of power from the Crownstone, will be so great that she may not survive it."

"May not survive? There's a chance she might die?"

Jack shook his head. "It would be better if she did not survive. Her soul. her spirit, would be burned out and utterly destroyed. Her body might live on but as an empty shell, mindless and unable to think or act. Life would be no more than a wakeful death."

It was a full minute before John could speak. "Then we've got to stop him!" he cried desperately. "We've got to!"

"And we shall try," said Corantyn, "or die in the attempt. It still remains for us to find the means."

The tinner's face clouded in thought. "Then here I will leave you," he said. "What is in my mind may be no more than the birth of an idea, but worth pursuing nonetheless. It was something you said, John, which compels me to look to the east for an answer." He turned to Corantyn. "Return to Castle Treryn, Corantyn. Search old Merlin's records: there must be something there of help. Unless I send word to the contrary, meet me at Chysauster at sunset."

"Time grows more precious by the second, my friend."

"I know it, son of Gwalchmai. Have faith."

14: SHALL TIMES
INTERMINGLE

JOHN watched as Jack of the Hammer rode swiftly away across the moor, taking the ancient ridgeway track called the Tinners' Way, until he was out of sight. "What do we do now?" he asked.

"As the tinner suggests," Corantyn replied, "we ride for Treryn Dinas. While he follows the instruction of the oracle, we must search through the old annals. The books and scrolls of Merlin Ambrosius have remained at Castle Treryn since his death. The tinner may well be right: the answer might be there."

They rode off by one of Corantyn's many secret routes. A thin haze lined the sky so that the horizon took on a watery look. Above them, though, the sky remained almost cloudless. The breeze had dropped considerably and, in other circumstances, it would have been a perfect summer's day.

"I will tell you a tale," said Corantyn, drawing his horse alongside John's pony. "It will make our journey even shorter, and you may learn a little more of our world in the telling of it.

"Long centuries past, and far from the Island of Britain, there once lay the realm of Asgard, home of the northern gods known as the Aesir. Some of those gods may be known to you even now, for they were much famed: Thor, master of thunder; Great

Father Odinn; Baldur the Fair; Loki Mischief-maker. Among their number was Weland, son of Wade, blacksmith of the Aesir. He it was who fashioned their weapons and armour, and there were none who could equal his skill.

"Asgard was growing ever weaker, for it had been foretold to the warlike Aesir that within a few centuries – and a century was but a moment to them – a new power would rise and eclipse them: a god of kindness and peace who would appear on Earth near the land of the Saracens and live for a while among men. They knew that as this Christos grew, so Asgard would diminish; an inevitability they had no choice but to accept.

"One by one, the Aesir assumed human form; turned their backs on godhood and walked among the peoples of the world. Weland the Smith chose to visit Britain for he was fascinated by the tales he had heard of this land. So he came and rested at a great barrow which stood amid a grove of trees, high on a hill on the southern Ridgeway. It was a peaceful and solitary place, much to his liking, and he was content to remain there for many years. He became known to those who travelled the Ridgeway as a strange and silent smith who was willing to shoe their horses for a small fee. His skill was such that his name spread far and wide and, to this day, they call the place Wayland's Smithy.

"There he stayed until the day he shod the horses of a merchant who told him of the headland of tin which lay at the very end of the land, towards the sunset. Weland's curiosity was whetted and he left the barrow to seek out this fabled land of tin.

"To forsake godhood and become, in his way, man, proved a fearful strain, even for one such as him. For the first time in his life, Weland fell sick. It was a fierce and desperate illness; his memory fled and he aimlessly wandered the wilderness of Dartmoor. He was found and tended by the ageing chieftain, Dart, who adopted Weland as his own son, for he had none. Weland no longer knew his own name, so Dart gave him another. Later, after his memory had returned, Weland decided to keep his new name: it was not uncommon and thus gave him the anonymity he desired. He never forgot his debt to old Dart and, even after resuming his search for the tin grounds, he returned many times with gifts to ensure that the old man wanted for nothing during the few years left to him.

"So, at last, Weland the Smith came to the tinfields of Belerion and struck up a strong friendship with the chieftain Tomas Hyr, or Long Tom. With Weland's skills to guide them, the two discovered many new tin lodes and better ways of working and smelting the metal, and both they and the people of Belerion became the richer for it.

"Of course, Weland was still an immortal and yet, by making himself man, he had developed man's emotions. He fell deeply in love with Genevra, Tom's eldest daughter, wed her and fathered a large family. There are many families of West Cornwall today who can find a common ancestor in Weland the Smith.

"Shortly before his wedding to Genevra, he came against the powers of a feared sorcerer, a certain Lord of Pengersek who, after the death of his own wife, coveted Long Tom's tin, wealth and daughter. He achieved nothing, for Weland was wilier than he, and it was soon after this defeat that Pengersek was to vanish from the burning wreck of his castle.

"Weland went on to thrive, yet still managed to keep his true identity secret from all. As his wife aged so he altered his own appearance as though he too was growing old with her. For his family he built a strong fortress, both to house them and to store and smelt the precious tin, safe from the pirates who were wont to raid the coast.

"The remains of that fortress lie on yonder hill-top, and is known as Chûn Castle."

John caught a curious gleam in the elf's eyes as he continued. "As for Weland, after the death of Genevra, he reverted to his favourite guise and has wandered Britain ever since. Usually, he will be seen as a young man in a strange coat fashioned from the hide of a young black bull; he who was once the god who forged Mjöllnir the Great, hammer of Thor, and who, even today, bears the twin of that hammer in his belt."

John's mouth sagged open as he realised the significance of what Corantyn had said, and he recalled the fury of the man who had discovered that the sorcerer's lair was none other than Chûn

Castle: the fortress he himself had built more than two thousand years before.

They were now climbing the flank of Dry Carn and could clearly see how well the site of the castle had been chosen. It commanded a vast area of land and had extensive views in all directions, including a wide vista of the coast. So well was it sited that only in the thickest moorland mist could anyone have approached it unseen.

Dry Carn, with its strange contrast of ancient and modern technology – at all Bronze Age menhir and a curious flying-saucer-like aircraft radar beacon - was itself a fine viewpoint. From a height of over seven hundred feet they looked down into a boggy, bowl-shaped valley, overlooked by the crags of Carn Kenidjack, and in the distance was St Just. Beyond that, stretching into the haze, lay the Atlantic.

But something didn't seem quite right to John. There was nothing he could put his finger on, yet something in the air around him had changed, subtly and almost imperceptibly. He blinked. The daylight seemed to flicker briefly like a faulty lamp. Corantyn reined in, sitting bolt upright in his saddle.

The light flickered again.

"What's going on?" John's own voice sounded distant, even to himself. Gawen was peering round suspiciously, his frowning eyes searching for something that none of them could see.

It came without further warning. The entire sky suddenly flashed a brilliant crimson, then again in orange, yellow, green, and on through all the colours of the spectrum. The horses whinnied in fear; Corantyn and Gawen fought to control their plunging mounts and John's pony reared under him, flinging him into the middle of a gorse bush. There was a moment of utter darkness before normal daylight returned to the world.

"Are you hurt, lad?" said Gawen.

John picked himself gingerly from the bush, pulling sharp green spines from his body. "I don't think so," he grinned ruefully. "Funny, though, I could've sworn that bush wasn't there just now." The dwarf chuckled and handed him back the reins of his pony.

"Where are we?" John asked.

Gawen drew a sharp breath and glanced rapidly around him. Corantyn wore a slight frown, and there was strain in his features.

The scattered farms had gone. No longer did St Just sit above its valley. The field patterns below them were different and smaller. The valley was choked with oak and alder, and yet it was unmistakeably the same valley, overlooked by the stark tor of Carn Kenidjack.

John's eyes turned fearfully in the direction of Chûn Castle, almost knowing what he would see. The granite walls reared from the hill-top, dominating the landscape: the outer some twelve feet high and surrounded by a rock-cut ditch; the inner, twice as tall, thick and impregnable. The staggered gateways were barred by great doors of nail-studded timber.

"Again the prophecy," said Corantyn. "'Shall Times Intermingle.' This is the Belerion of the sixth century."

"We've gone back in time!" John exclaimed.

"I think it is not so simple," the elf replied thoughtfully. "Say rather that times have moved together. The twentieth century is here, all around us, but we can neither see nor touch it. I have heard of such things and know that the dimensions of time and space are unstable. There is a curtain between the times: it is tenuously thin and there will be momentary gaps for those who can find them. Nonetheless it has happened, and fulfilled a further line of the prophecy."

"And yet another," interrupted Gawen. "Turn your eyes to the south, my friends. The Golowan fires burn on Bartinnê."

Two miles away, the bulk of Bartinnê Hill heaved its brown dome above the surrounding moor and, from its lofty summit, three plumes of white smoke spiralled high into the air, where fires were greeting the sun.

THE summit of Bartinnê was crowned by a peculiar earthwork, circular in shape and about eighty paces across. The single enclosing bank had no external ditch and was low, scarcely more than a man's height, with its inner face fashioned into rows of rough seats. Three small ring banks, edged with stone slabs, lay in the centre and in each a great furze fire crackled and blazed, sending dense columns of smoke into the sky.

The place was filled with people in robes and headdresses of the palest blue.One of a small group near the centre bore a huge, sheathed ceremonial sword, while another carried a curving horn which he put to his lips as John, Gawen and Corantyn entered the enclosure. A loud, clear note echoed and lingered on the soft breeze. Immediate silence followed, while all eyes turned to the newcomers.

The gathering included men and women of all ages. A man wearing ornate trappings of beaten and highly polished copper and evidently their leader, was particularly remarkable.

He was old but his body was as firm and upright as that of an athlete. He was extremely tall and his bearded face, though lined, had a young man's eyes, keen and grey, but filled with the knowledge and wisdom of long ages. From the headpiece which, like his outer robe, was of a much deeper blue than those of his fellows and inlaid with gold embroidery, spilled locks of silver hair, and his white beard was long and full with a darker, iron-grey streak on either side of the chin. His nose was hooked like the beak of a bird of prey. John thought he heard Corantyn catch his breath

"What is all this?" John began, but Gawen warned him to silence.

"Have respect," he said softly. "This is a high and ancient gathering: the Gorseth of the Bards of Cornwall. This is their Midsummer gathering but, if I am not mistaken, they also meet for us. Or rather, I think, for you."

"For me?" John started, but his question was stilled by the voice of the Grand Bard. Turning to the bard who held the great horn, he commanded:

"*Dhe Gernow, Kernyas, wheth dha Gorn. Ha'n clewer yn hy feswar sorn . . . yn Hanow Dew!*"

The horner turned to east, south, west and north, winding the horn to each of the four cardinal points.

"*An Gwyr erbyn an Bys,*" intoned the old man. "The Truth against the World." He motioned the trio to dismount, and three Bardic marshals stepped forward to take their horses.

John glanced quickly at Corantyn, who whispered: "He will

call three times for peace. Keep silence until he speaks to you, for I believe he will."

The powerful voice of the Grand Bard rang out: "*Unwyth orthough ywhovynnaf: Us Cres?*"

A great cry erupted from the blue-robed assembly; two hundred voices raised as one: "*Cres!*"

"*Dywwyth orthough y whovynnaf: Us Cres?*"

"*Cres!*"

"*Tergwyth orthough y whovynnaf: Us Cres?*"

"*Cres!*"

The Grand Bard beckoned the boy forward, motioned that he should remain standing, then took his hands and held them firmly together between his own.

"John Trevelyan, we welcome thee to this gathering of the Gorseth of Kernow. We welcome also Corantyn, son of Farinmail, elf-lord of Castle Treryn, who is well known to me. Also Gawen the warrior, son of Gwalchmai, whose heart is as true as his axe-blade is sharp."

"My friends, you go to Castle Treryn to search its records of Merlin? Then I tell you, that the search would be in vain."

He gazed down at John's bowed head, and said softly

> " 'In days ever strange to the cry of the horn
> Shall Times Intermingle and bright shine a Stone
> Two innocent ones, of a midsummer morn
> Shall unlock the portals, old memories be known,
> A Raven be summoned, and fires greet the sun;
> By the Dark Hour of Witchcraft shall these deeds be done.' "

John looked sharply up into the old man's eyes. "You have heard this?" said the Grand Bard. The boy nodded wordlessly.

"And the second verse: is that known to you?"

John shook his head. "Then I shall recite. Listen well, John Trevelyan, for it was, in part, written for you:

> 'Venture in peril, O son of the Lords,
> For the weapon of he whose love was his end
> In the face of the deep shall ye brandish the Sword;

The fell ones shall ride and the Dark One defend
Daemon rides daemon, a battle be fought,
At the Dark Hour of Witchcraft, a victory bought.' "

"Written for me?" John stared at the old man. "But what does it mean?"

"You are the youngest male descendant of the direct line of the Lord Trevelyan, therefore it is you who is the 'son of the Lords'. That much is clear, and as you are such, a task awaits you. If you are to have hope, then you must claim 'the weapon of he whose love was his end'. I know of this weapon, and where it may be found. It is a sword which lies within the land of your forefathers: the land of Lyonesse. It is there you must seek it."

"But how? The Lyonesse doesn't exist any more. It's at the bottom of the sea."

The old man smiled a curious smile. "At the bottom of the sea," he murmured. "Come, John Trevelyan, and see for yourself."

Baffled, John followed the Grand Bard's long strides to the entrance of the Bardic enclosure. It faced south-west and the distant sea lay hidden beneath the summer haze. The old man stretched out his right arm, swinging it in a slow, horizontal arc from left to right.

The curtain of the haze cleared back as if swept aside. To north and south, the intense blue of the Atlantic Ocean glinted in the sun but, to the west, stretching away in folds of brown and green to the shadowy hills on the horizon, lay the legend itself in all its beauty and splendour: the land, no longer lost, of Lyonesse.

15: THE LOST LAND

IT seemed an age before John could tear his eyes away from the incredible sight; the green, low-lying land where there should have been sea, from the grey bluff of the Land's End to the misty heights in the far distance.

"Do you really mean that I have to go there?" he said finally. His voice trembled.

The Grand Bard gazed at him with solemn eyes. "The prophecy so demands," he answered.

"On my own?"

"It must be so, John Trevelyan. The verse speaks of you, and no other. While it chiefly foretells, those lines are also a distinct instruction. To stray from them in any way would it be too much to risk. The son of the Lords, and only he, can succeed in this quest.

"I have studied the words of the Belerion Prophecy and know that the sword you must seek is like no other, save one, and that is no longer part of this world. The sword of the verse is a wondrous blade; the hilt is richly wrought and set with jewels beyond price, while the blade itself shines with a blue light which is not that of earthly iron."

He pointed a long, gnarled finger. "Halfway between here and the Heights of Syllan is a tall hill and at its foot lies the town of

Lethowsa, capital of the Lyonesse. From the town, a road climbs to the citadel on the hill-top. This is a strong fortress; its name is Caer Trygva, and you will find the sword within. This is all I may tell you. Perform this task well, son of Trevelyan; your sister's life depends on you."

John looked again at the lost land of Lyonesse. He noticed that it was not joined to the mainland, but sundered from it by a shallow channel between the Land's End and the craggy ridge which, in other days, would be a jagged reef, perpetually surrounded by surging water and watched over by the slim pencil of the Longships lighthouse. From his high viewpoint he could clearly pick out the winding track from the tidal ford to Lethowsa and, as he committed its route to memory, he again went over the instructions of the Grand Bard.

He shrugged with reluctant acceptance. "I suppose I'd better get going, then." he said, moving towards his pony.

Corantyn helped John up into the saddle, and gave him the reins. "Go now, John, and with all speed. Only twelve hours remain to us. Come back safely and remember that all our thoughts ride with you."

John looked down into the faces and saw the thinly concealed strain which lay behind them. He was on his own and he realised that everything, including the life of his sister, depended solely on him. There could be no turning aside, no turning back, even though the unknown lay ahead. He swung the horse around, waved once, and rode away down the hill-side towards the legend that awaited him.

THE tough pony had carried him for more than an hour at a steady canter and showed little sign of tiring. So far, the way had been easy; the road clear and the terrain fairly level. He had seen no other travellers; in fact he had seen no one at all.

He reined in on the crest of a low ridge and found himself looking into a shallow, but sheltered, valley. There, before his eyes, lay the town of Lethowsa.

John was surprised. He had expected to find a town of rich, elegant buildings, pillared and marbled, with wide paved streets bustling with exotic people, as in pictures of other sunken lands like Atlantis. Instead, he found a ghost town; a deserted collection of rough stone huts and houses, some small and round with cone-shaped thatched roofs, while others were large and oval, each with a number of rooms opening into a central, unroofed courtyard, paved with flat, unhewn slabs. The roads that led into the town and between the low buildings were little more than dusty, rutted tracks. Lethowsa was not large by any means. Perhaps there were less than fifty separate buildings in the settlement which, along with its surrounding fields, was set in a large clearing of the woodland that encircled it.

Like the countryside he had just ridden through, everything was far too quiet and still. Fields and pastures were empty of livestock, and no people walked the dusty streets. There were no voices, no sounds of work, and no birdsong.

John rode slowly through the deserted town, taking note of the open gates and doors. His eyes glanced from side to side, ever watchful for the slightest movement, but there was none. He shivered in spite of himself. It was as if he were the only living soul left in the land, and yet he could feel that curious, uncomfortable sensation which told him that there was someone who watched and waited.

He forced the thought to the back of his mind and rode on through the township to the track leading up to the hill-top fortress; a massive, single wall which encircled the summit, linking outcrop to outcrop of solid, unyielding granite. There were seven of them; huge, natural towers of rock. John dismounted in front of the closed fortress gates.

A yellowish tint had crept into the sky and angry clouds towered menacingly above the horizon. John did not like the look of them, but focused his attention on the massive gates of Caer Trygva; timber double doors which were set well back in a deeply recessed entranceway.

He steeled himself, took a deep breath and knocked boldly. No one came, no voice called out. He knocked again, louder and louder. "Is anyone there?" he shouted. Still there was no reply, and John sucked at his sore knuckles. Then he gave the doors a shove, and to his surprise they swung easily open at his touch. He hovered uncertainly, then stepped cautiously in.

Like the town below, the fort was empty. No guards stalked the battlements and no voices challenged his intrusion. In the centre of the fort stood a large rectangular building of timber, quite unlike anything he'd seen in the town below. This too had double doors, but these stood invitingly open. John walked purposefully towards them, still expecting at any moment to hear a shout of challenge.

He stopped suddenly. From somewhere to his right, perhaps from one of the stone buildings which lined the inside of the great wall, had come the unmistakeable snort of a horse. He stood still, waiting for a repeat of the sound, but heard nothing more. He walked on to the open doors of the hall and stepped inside.

It was dimly lit, and the high roof was supported by ranks of stout wooden pillars. As far as John could tell, the hall was empty except for a large unhewn block of granite, which stood on a square plinth in the centre of the room. Beams of light, filtering down from a small square opening in the roof, fell upon the stone, and on the great sword that lay on its flat top.

The blade was unsheathed and lay beside its ornate scabbard. The hilt was jewel-studded and, where the light played on the naked blade, its bluish glint was unmistakeable.

'All I have to do is pick it up and go,' John thought excitedly. 'There's no one here to stop me.' He moved eagerly forward, stepping quickly onto the stone plinth and reaching out for the sword.

"Who dares to claim the Sword of Tears?" The hollow voice came from nowhere, filling the hall with echoes and stopping John in his tracks.

"Who's there?" he shouted fearfully, the echo of his words fleeing among the high rafters.

"I am the appointed Guardian of the Sword." The solemn words seemed to veil an unspoken threat.

John's eyes, adjusting slowly to the gloom, roved around the hall, seeking out the source of the voice. A man stepped from the shadows of a dark corner. He was richly robed in dark red, and a hood shadowed the whole of his face except for the tip of a trim, iron-grey beard.

The Guardian placed a reverend hand on the richly decorated hilt. "This is Dagrenou, Sword of Tears, once the weapon of Tristan the Sorrowful."

Words from the prophecy burned through the boy's mind: ' . . . the weapon of he whose love was his end . . . ' Tristan and Esselt. Tristan of Lyonesse.

The Guardian went on. "Note you well the hue of its blade. This is not of earthly iron, but of iron sent from the heavens. Thus given by God, and forged with skill, it is great in power. Only one other such blade has ever existed and that is Caledvol'h, the sword of Arthur the Soldier, Count of Britain.

"Why have you come here, boy? Mayhap to steal, but you are young and curiously clad for an ordinary thief."

John ignored the accusation, but not the voice. It was strangely familiar. He was sure he had heard it before but, try as he might, he couldn't place it. He looked up at the tall figure, trying to peer under the hood, but the shadows were too deep. John decided to answer the question by asking another.

"Do you know the Belerion Prophecy?" he asked.

The man stiffened, drawing a swift breath through clenched teeth. "Is it you?" he uttered, then, after a long pause, "Are you the Son of the Lords?"

John evaded the question. "The Bards at Bartinnê sent me. They said that I must obey the prophecy; that I must find the sword and take it back to them."

"And whose hand shall wield it? Who is the warrior of such worth?"

"I . . . I don't know," he said lamely. He thought hard, then, with an unexpected flash of inspiration: "Rialobran – maybe it's for him."

The effect of Rialobran's name on the Guardian was startling: "The Prince of Belerion! Then truly he must face the Shadow. Indeed he is a man worthy to take up the Sword of Tears and yet – where is the proof that you are what you claim and not an emissary of evil?"

"Proof?" John stared at him helplessly. "I haven't got any proof. What sort of proof do you want?"

"There is a way." The Guardian of the Sword seemed to loom

menacingly over him. "Do you take up the Sword of Tristan, but I give you dire warning. Should you be of the legions of evil, the sword will surely slay you as you grasp it." His gloved hand indicated the fabulous blade. "There lies the sword you seek. Take it, if you have the courage."

John bit his lip and gazed at the sword. Then, with a sudden, decisive movement, he reached out and firmly gripped the gem-studded hilt. He looked defiantly into the shadowed face, lifted the sword, slid it into its sheath and buckled it around his shoulders.

The Guardian made no attempt to stop him but, instead, nodded thoughtfully. "Then truly you have the right to take it to Belerion. I commend your boldness, for I spoke in truth. Should you have been sent by those who serve the Shadow, you would, even now, be lying slain – " He broke off, glancing up sharply. A piece of thatch fluttered down from the roof and, beneath their feet, the ground trembled ever so slightly.

"So soon . . . !" the Guardian muttered to himself. "Must it be so soon?"

But John didn't hear him. A nervous, fear-filled whinny rang out and, with a cry of panic, the boy turned and ran from the building. He was too late. Even before he had reached the fortress gates, the pony, sensing danger, had torn herself loose and fled.

"No!" John yelled frantically, "wait! WAIT!" But his mount had gone, her fear and sense of survival sending her streaking back across the plain of Lyonesse, towards the distant hills of Belerion.

A second tremor, stronger than the first, shook the ground and small stones pattered down from the great wall. The sky was now obscured by massive formations of cloud and there was a distant ripple of thunder

John dashed back to the dark hall, shouting for the Guardian, searching its shadowy corners, but the strange hooded man had vanished as mysteriously as he had appeared. John was alone

Racking his brains, he recalled the horse he'd heard earlier and rushed outside to search the buildings which lined the fortress wall. He ran from house to house, looking frantically in each

He reached out and firmly gripped the gem-studded hilt

one, but found nothing but empty silence. Only a scatter of hay in a vacant stall remained to show that any beast had ever been there. Forlorn, he stood in the middle of the deserted hill fort, filled with despair. There was no other choice: whether he liked it or not, he now faced the prospect of walking the long miles back to Belerion, and the hours were ticking away.

IT was as well that John was young and fit. By walking and jogging in turn, he covered more than five miles in less than an hour, but he was tiring fast and barely halfway to the mainland. The earth tremors were increasing in both frequency and strength and the ground under his feet was beginning to lurch like an unbroken colt. Just the effort of keeping his balance was a drain on his stamina, as was the weight of the sword.

At one point, he had seen a band of riders, perhaps two hundred strong, heading westward at speed. With the exception of the Guardian of the sword, these were the first people he had seen in the Lyonesse, but their direction and intent indicated that they had come from the mainland. None appeared to have seen him; for some reason they had abandoned the winding road and taken a straight course across country. They did not come within a quarter of a mile of him, but pursued their course towards the distant western hills, looking neither left nor right.

His ears began to hurt. There had been a sudden change in the pressure of the air. He held his nose and blew to clear his ears. They popped painfully and returned to normal. Now he could hear the rising sound of a rushing wind and, in the distance, trees were beginning to wave violently.

Suddenly an invisible wall of wind hit him like a solid fist; a terrific force which hurled him to the ground where he lay in terror, the air roaring and howling around him. There was an awful sound of tearing and rending anda nearby oak, its roots forcibly ripped from the ground, keeled over and fell with a terrible crash. Then, as quickly as it had come, the wind had gone, leaving an eerie moan which faded away into the distance.

John clambered painfully to his feet. The air had now become uncannily still and silence had fallen on the lost land. The dark underside of the heavy cover of cloud was curiously shot with red.

Yet another tremor rippled the ground. Seconds later he heard a throaty rumble and, a couple of hundred yards away, the ground split open and a fountain shot high into the air; not a fountain of water, but of liquid fire. Magma from the foundations of the earth had found and forced its way through and, within minutes, more fissures appeared, each belching its crimson spout.

John broke into a run. The hills of Penwith, even the rugged bluff he knew as the Land's End, seemed a world away. His heart suddenly leapt into his mouth and he battled to stop as a huge cleft opened without warning, directly in his path. He threw himself backwards, slithering and sliding, clawing desperately for something to clutch. His grasping fingers closed on a clump of grass, his eyes screwed shut: beneath his feet was a sickening emptiness.

One frail tuft of grass had somehow halted his mad slide and he lay on his side with his feet dangling over the abyss. He drew quickly back to solid ground. Crawling gingerly to the edge, he craned his neck to see what lay below. The sides of the fissure funnelled down into darkness but, far below, a glimmer of red flickered briefly. John looked around for another path, but there was none. His only choice was to leap the chasm.

'It's nothing!' he told himself, out loud. 'Only six or seven feet. Any fool can jump across that!' But six or seven feet is not so easily leapt in the knowledge that one slip would mean a certain and horrible death.

He backed away, steadied himself and, with a surge of courage born of desperation, sprinted forward and leapt. His eyes were tightly shut as his toes hit solid ground, and he pitched forward, outflung hands clutching fistfuls of earth.

A quivering rumble from deep in the earth brought him scrambling to his feet. By now he'd seen enough to know what it meant and he raced to where a group of boulders offered a possible shelter. He dived headfirst over the rocks, landing in an untidy heap with the pommel of the sword poking painfully into his ribs. He rolled back, pressing himself hard against the granite boulder.

A broken wall of flame and molten rock shot high into the air from the fissure some fifty yards behind. John pressed himself even harder into the rock as fiery fragments pitched uncomfortably close, and his nostrils flinched at the stench of sulphur. Nevertheless, he stayed firmly where he was until the eruption subsided, then got up and walked uneasily away.

He frowned. The constant rumbling had subtly altered its tone, and was growing steadily louder. He paused, cocking his head to listen. The sound didn't appear to be coming from the ground; neither did it sound like thunder or wind. It was more like . . .

Suddenly he knew, and his stomach churned at the horror of it. Almost in slow motion he turned, and sank slowly to his knees at the terror of seeing the manner of his own death.

16: VISIONS

PENNY slept. She lay on a raised couch of velvet around which burned four flames in shallow vessels set on stands of ornately worked iron; two at her head, two at her feet. Of this, or even of where she was, she knew nothing for she lay under a deep enchantment gently wrought by the potent harp-magic of the sorcerer.

Pengersek had done her no harm, nor could he, as he was constantly reminded by the threatening glow of the Crownstone at the girl's breast. Even in her trance-like sleep, Penny's mind was conscious of its protective warmth.

In fact, nothing could have been further from Pengersek's mind than the thought of harming the girl; she meant nothing to him other than the fact that she was the bearer of the stone, and was as insignificant as an ant. His only desire was the Crownstone itself and the power locked within it, but he could not touch it for it would destroy him instantly and utterly, as it would if he raised as much as a single finger of malice against its wearer, as he knew only too well.

Penny's sleep was a deep one and not without dreams, but the dreams which invaded her mind were not the usual confused images that are afterwards hard to recall. Instead, she was granted a series of visions, so real and so sharp that not a single detail would ever escape her memory. Beneath the spellbound sleep was a strange state of consciousness, which allowed her mind to see and to wonder, to question and remember.

At first, it seemed to her that she was standing on a bare moor where rugged tors loomed high above a scene of dreadful carnage. It was the aftermath of a battle; some terrible, merciless conflict that had left dead men and dead horses as far as her eyes could see. Death lay everywhere, bloody and grotesque.

But in the midst of all this destruction, there was still one tiny spark of life. Close at hand lay the body of a burly, powerful warrior; a man whose grey beard and lined features spoke of a life of many battles, of which this had been his last.

His helmet was beautifully fashioned in shining bronze, with hinged guards for nose, neck and ears, and its crest was the sinuous figure of a dragon, wings outspread and jaws agape, its neck arched back and ready to strike. Much of the man's body was enveloped in the folds of a cloak of deep purple, now torn and shredded, but she could see the fringe of a Roman-style battleskirt, leather leggings and high boots of polished hide. Glimpses of the breastplate of linked scales of bronze were also visible, and it was the slight movement of this, a faint flicker of the closed eyelids and the bursting of tiny bubbles of crimson froth at the corners of the mouth that betrayed the tenuous presence of life. She could not see the old warrior's wound, but the grass beneath his head was sodden with blood.

Three men stepped into her line of vision, and that one of them was obviously a leader of some kind was evident by the way his companions bowed and fawned around him. Penny disliked him at first sight. He was thin and wiry, not above thirty years of age, and his face held the look of a hungry rat. His head was heavily bound with torn rags through which blood slowly seeped. The man's eyes were wild and staring; the eyes of a madman.

All three were clothed in a similar fashion to the stricken warrior round whom they gathered, although the helmets worn by the two of lesser rank were plainer and their cloaks duller and of rougher material. Beneath her enchanted slumber, Penny's mind was already beginning to pose questions. What era was she seeing? Which battle was this and what connection, if any, did it have with herself?

The rat-faced leader spoke; a harsh voice which broke the stillness like a whiplash. "Casvallon, examine the body. See if he is truly dead at long last."

The man called Casvallon knelt over the fallen warrior's body, holding his ear close to the grey-bearded mouth. He looked up and there was wonder in his face.

"He lives, Lord Medraut! I can hardly believe it. Can any man take such a wound and survive? His end must be close; shall I hasten his departure?" His fingers strayed to his sword-hilt, but a quick movement of Medraut's hand stopped him.

"Touch him not. Such mercy is weakness. As you say, he will soon be dead, and no man's hand will have slain him but mine." He laughed cruelly. "My hand, Casvallon! Not even Cerdic the Saxon could have achieved that. Let all men remember that here on the field of Camlann, I, Medraut, became the man who slew the mighty Arthur!"

Penny's mind reeled at those words. So this had been the final tragic battle of Camlann. The man with the twisted mind and madman's eyes was the traitor Medraut, while the old, dying warrior was none other than the great warlord of Celtic Britain, Arthur himself.

Medraut looked away, then turned again with a sharp movement which brought a brief spasm of agony to his face.

"Caledvol'h!" he cried shrilly. "Where is the sword Caledvol'h? How can I become Warlord of Britain without the sword which he bore, and Aurelianus before him, and Maximus long ago? Where is it? Where is the sword, curse you?" The voice became a deranged scream.

The third man spoke softly. "Bedwyr took it, lord. He and a score of Arthur's men took the sword and fled westward. They are all that is left."

Medraut rounded on him. "Bedwyr . . . Arthur's lieutenant? You let him live? You let him take the sword?" The voice, which had begun to scream again, calmed unpredictably. "Then we must follow. They rode west, you say? Down through the length of Kernyw to the Lyonesse, and what lies beyond that but the sea? Let them flee, for we shall follow: they have nowhere to go, nowhere to hide. How many are we?"

"Twice a hundred, lord, or thereabouts."

Medraut pursed his lips and drew them into a savage grin. "And just a score of them, to die on our spears or be driven into the sea. Either way, I'll have that sword and an end to all resistance. Come, we'll waste no more time here."

The ears of Penny's mind heard the thunder of Medraut's cavalry diminish into the west, and she turned again to look at the fallen figure of Arthur. He was no longer there

THERE was no time for her to wonder at this, for the scene changed to a little stone-built hermit's cell, ivy-clad and almost hidden amidst the bracken and tangled thorn of a flattish landscape. Penny instantly recognised the hills in the distance as Chapel Carn Brea, Bartinnê and Brane, which rose to the north of St Buryan. Outside the open door of the cell stood a foam-flecked horse, bow-necked and untethered, too exhausted to react to the arrival of Medraut and his army.

Medraut himself, unsteady from fatigue and the effects of his wound, dismounted and entered the dim cell. There was a simple straw pallet in the corner and on it lay the body of a warrior, a youngish man no older than Medraut. The arms had been crossed on the chest and the still, dead face was at peace.

The traitor's eyes widened as he started forward. "Alun!" he breathed. "Oh, Alun, we were as brothers in our youth so long ago. Your loyalty lay ever with Arthur: now death is your only reward. I am not so eaten with hatred that I cannot pray for your soul."

"Pray, Medraut?" An ancient, bowed man, dressed in a simple habit, shuffled from a dark corner. The front of his head was shaved, but long, white hair hung down his back. "Pray? Thy very presence defiles this shrine to the gentle saint Beryana. Make thy peace with this comrade ye have murdered; make thy peace quickly. Then take thyself from this shrine, traitor."

Medraut stiffened, turning his wild eyes to the hermit-priest.

"Aye!" said the old man. "Traitor! Both to God and to Man art thou traitor!"

Medraut whirled, smashing the back of his open hand viciously into the hermit's face. The old man toppled, pitching backwards into the corner of the room. There was blood on his lips and he wiped it away.

"Courage indeed," he cried, "to strike thus an old and defenceless man. Go, Medraut! Face thy doom! Even now, the shade of a mighty one stands before thee! Ride on, Medraut! Ride on and die!"

Medraut glared down at the hermit and drew his sword halfway from its sheath. Then, with a snarl of anger, he slammed it back, spat full in the hermit's face and stalked from the cell.

It was a very different scene outside. His men were shouting in alarm as they struggled to control horses maddened with fear, and Medraut heard again the hermit's words: "The shade of a mighty one stands before thee!"

A stone's throw ahead of his army, a little column of cloud hung motionless in mid-air, unaffected by the breeze; ominous and somehow threatening. Medraut turned his back on it and, with difficulty, mounted his restless horse.

"Fools!" he shouted. "Ignore it! Tis only some petty phantasm conjured by yon dotard of a hermit. There is no power there, save to frighten children!"

The warriors, in dread of the ghostly cloud, but more so of their crazed leader, moved on in his wake towards the Lyonesse and, as they moved, so the misty column moved before them, always maintaining a constant distance ahead.

The scene dissolved

NOW, Penny saw a rugged cove set deep beneath the dark crags of a great promontory that was joined to the mainland only by a high, razor-thin neck of rock. There were many low buildings on the headland, both on its flat top and on high ledges of the cliff, and people were making their way down precarious paths to the stony beach. All were solemn; many wept silently.

A black-sailed boat lay in the cove, and six men, bearing a litter on their shoulders, moved slowly up the lowered gangplank. They laid the litter gently onto the deck of the boat, barely stirring the body which lay upon it.

By some miracle, Arthur still clung onto life, and his eyes were open, gazing up at the nearest of three hooded women who knelt beside him. She was perhaps even older than he was but the fine structure of her face told of the beauty it had once had. She put out a gentle hand of restraint as Arthur tried to raise his head and his words were little more than a broken whisper.

"Morgan . . . Morgan, my sister. So it has ended, here at Tintagel where it all began, so many, many years ago."

"Hush, brother. Be still and take comfort, for it is not yet ended. We have come to bear you away from men, to Enys Avallen where, in time, this wound will heal. There in the island valley shall you rest and grow again to strength and youth, in readiness for the day when your Celtic people shall once more be in need of your leadership."

Arthur lay back his grey head, smiling softly.

PENNY knew that she was now being shown the land of Lyonesse; a Lyonesse of sullen skies that resounded to the rumble of Medraut's army. The strange column of mist was still there in front of them, its speed exactly matching that of the relentless cavalry.

One of Medraut's officers was shouting, pointing a jubilant finger. "There, Lord Medraut! Bedwyr's troop, high on Syllan. See how their spears flash in the sun!"

Medraut laughed crazily. "Trapped! Nowhere to run but the wild ocean. We have them now. Caledvol'h is as good as mine already!"

Another man cried out, his voice edged with fear. "Look, the cloud! It changes shape!"

The army clattered to an uncertain halt while Medraut sat like a mounted statue, his deranged eyes staring at the cloud as it descended slowly until it touched the ground, where it shrank, took form, solidified. Then there stood before them the hazy figure of a tall, upright old man, bald headed, hook nosed and full-bearded. Recognition among the soldiers was voiced in terror.

"Merlin! It is Merlin!"

"Merlin's dead!"

"His ghost has come to avenge Arthur!"

"Silence, fools!" screamed Medraut. "What can the shade of a dead prophet achieve against those who slew Arthur?" He glared at the silent phantom. "Arthur is dead! Dead, do you hear? There is a new Warlord of Britain now, and the dead have no dominion over Medraut the Great. Hear me, Merlinus Ambrosius: I defy you!"

There was no reply. The calm eyes of Merlin gazed sadly at the traitor. For a full minute they stared at each other, the silence pressing in on them, until the wizard raised his arms, stretching them out sideways, level with his shoulders. Then he turned his gnarled hands upwards so that the palms faced the sky.

A tremendous peal of thunder shattered the quiet and forked lightnings speared down from the heavy clouds. The ground muttered, heaved and split open in a thousand places. Fire and lava belched from the broken earth and the underbelly of the clouds glowed like molten copper.

Again the wizard turned his palms to the sky. The earth gave a long, horrible groan and began to subside in a confusion of sound.

Medraut screamed in terror while his army, wailing horribly, tried in vain to turn and flee. Men were flung headlong from their terrified mounts as the sea rushed in on them.

Pictures came thick and fast into Penny's mind. A giant oak lurched in the grip of a mighty blast of wind, heeled over and crashed in splinters. Out on the plain, a solitary rider on a white horse galloped with incredible speed towards the hills of Penwith, and a small figure carrying a huge sword stood helplessly in the path of the onrushing wave.

It looked like John. Surely it couldn't be . . . no, that was silly. What Penny was seeing had taken place one and a half thousand years ago.

There was one last, awful sight: the screaming face of Medraut, blood streaming from the gaping wound in his skull. Then he was gone, whirled away forever by the raging force of the Atlantic.

HER dream was not yet over. A handful of exhausted men stood high on a windy cliff top, gazing in stunned silence at the swirling, churning sea which, in a matter of moments, had drowned an entire country. That ocean, a storm-wracked stretch of water flowing above a lost legend, would be there for all time, while the hill on which they stood, and those which lay close by, would forever be islands.

"And now, Bedwyr?" said one of the men. "What is left for us?"

Bedwyr, like Arthur, his kinsman and commander, was old for a warrior, as were most of the small group. He gazed tearfully at the savage sea before glancing down at the great sword he held in his right hand.

"The book," he said quietly, "is closed, Owain, but for us another has begun. The age of Arthur is over. The Lyonesse is destroyed and Medraut, too, has gone . . . and yet, by God's good grace, we have been delivered.

"We grow old, all of us. During our lives, we did what we could to stem the darkness. We are too old and too few to save Britain from the Saxons now. I fear for the young; there is no time to rebuild and no one to lead. Nevermore will there be a Warlord of Britain. Now, Owain, even Caledvol'h's story has come to an end for there is no one to inherit it. – I shall remain here on these new islands and raise a house to God in thanks for our salvation. The few years left to me will I spend in His service."

"How many years have we all been together, Bedwyr, be it in war or peace?" said Owain. "It is not for us to desert you now. It will be a new and different life for all of us, a new challenge; but let us meet it together, companions of Arthur and servants of God."

Bedwyr smiled wistfully. "I am glad, Owain. Now let us put an end to what is past." He studied the legendary sword, savouring the memories it recalled. "I have heard it said that Caledvol'h was brought from the waters long ago. Let us now return it, and go in peace."

He strapped Arthur's sword into its richly wrought scabbard, then whirled and flung it with all his might away from the cliff. The sword arched downward, a hundred feet and more, twisting and turning in the air so that the jewels of hilt and scabbard glittered as it fell; a curving trail of fire to the ocean far below.

A pale hand rose from the waves, deftly catching the weapon below the hilt. Three times it brandished the sword and, on the third movement, a solitary beam of sunlight caught it, so that it shone like a great Cross before the warriors-who-had-been; servants of Christ to be.

Then it was drawn beneath the sea, nevermore to be seen by man.

17: DELUGE

JOHN Trevelyan shook uncontrollably, his mind refusing to believe what his eyes were seeing. He now knew for certain how the Lyonesse had perished; how he himself was to die.

No wonder this land had been deserted. Its people must have read the signs and left for the mainland days earlier, and yet, for some reason the mysterious Guardian had remained, alone in an empty fort above the abandoned town. Now it was John who was alone, hopelessly marooned in the middle of the lost land, on foot and far from the mainland. Time had run out, and with it, all hope.

The wall of water racing in from the sea was a hundred feet high, a colossal curling lip capped with gleaming foam. It seemed to call to him: 'You have gambled, John Trevelyan . . . and you have lost. I come now to claim the debt!'

As if in a dream, he sensed a movement behind him, but the huge wave held his eyes, awed and mesmerised. Then a strong hand grasped his collar, hauling him, choking and gagging, into the air.

A harsh cry of command rang out, jolting him back to his senses, and John found that he was lying across the muscular shoulders of a great white horse. He twisted his neck to look up at the face of the rider . . . and the mad unreality went on.

The man's hair was long and dark, but greying at the temples. A circlet of bright metal, inscribed with many tiny words and set with a single green gemstone, adorned his head, and his beard was iron-grey. But the face was the face of Ben Trevelyan!

The great horse raced on at a speed John could hardly believe. Trees, rocks, fields, hedges; all appeared before them and flew past in a blur of colour. The ground steepened briefly and John glanced up to see the looming cliffs of what would become, at any moment, the Land's End. The ground dipped again and salt water sprayed up from the pounding hoofs as they sped across the shallow channel which separated the Lyonesse from the mainland. Their ears were filled with the deafening thunder of the sea. On the far side of the channel lay a long curve of white sand and, beyond it, the hill.

The rider was shouting, screaming at the horse, urging the great animal to a final surge of effort. Dry sand spurted up at them, then all was lost in a tremendous, shattering roar. The sea was upon them.

They shot forward, man, boy and horse, in a roaring bedlam of whirling green water. Stones pummelled and cut them, then the breath was driven from their bodies by a jarring crash that numbed John's senses. He panicked, striking out blindly, his empty lungs screaming for air.

Someone had once told him that drowning was a pleasant way to die, but John knew better. It was an awful, lingering death, filled with terror and darkness . . . He could hold on no longer: he had to breathe even though only the sea would fill his aching lungs. Resigned, yet relieved, he opened his mouth and breathed . . . fresh, sweet air!

He opened his eyes. A patch of blue smiled down from a break in the clouds. His fingers closed on wet grass and, between his own panting, rasping breaths, he heard a horse stamp and snort.

"We're alive!" he croaked. His rescuer ignored him. He sat beside the boy on the soaking turf of the hill-side, gazing silently down on a scene of utter destruction. A large droplet ran down the man's face. It might have been seawater from his hair; John thought it was a tear.

From the place where they sat to the western horizon was a boiling surge of water and steam. Debris of all kinds, mostly splintered trees, tossed up and down on the heaving waves. At one point, John thought he saw the body of a man being swept along in a swirling current, but it was a fleeting glimpse and then the figure was lost.

The hand of his rescuer suddenly gripped John's arm tightly. He turned, but the man was not looking at him. Instead, he was staring, intent and wide-eyed, at the sky.

It may only have been a freak of nature, but the clouds to the west seemed to be forming the shape of a face; old, bearded and wise, yet overwhelmed by a racking grief. The vision lingered for just a moment before fading.

"Merlin Ambrosius," murmured the rider. "So this is how it ends. Even in death he remains powerful. I saw the army of Medraut the False out there on the plain, and knew that Arthur had breathed his last." He sighed deeply.

Sick with horror, John turned his gaze back to the howling, churning sea. "How many people?" he whispered. "How many have died?"

The man from the Lyonesse shook his head slowly. "Only Medraut and his followers are dead. The fate of the Lyonesse was written long ago and there were signs in the stars which warned our astrologers. The people abandoned their country three days ago. I alone remained, for such was my duty. The Belerion prophecy was unfulfilled: the son of the Lords had yet to come, to claim the Sword of Tears, so I waited."

John caught his breath. "So you were the Guardian?"

The man said nothing as John went on. "But why did you leave me there? You knew my horse had bolted; you left me to walk back alone! You knew what was going to happen, I was left to die!"

The Guardian slowly turned his face towards him and again John saw the uncanny resemblance to Ben Trevelyan: even the voice was similar.

"No," said the Guardian, "I would not have let you die. Are you not alive now? I had seen your courage in the claiming of the sword Dagrenou; I had to see more. Do you not understand?"

John suddenly knew the question that was coming, and a curious thrill ran through him.

"Do you not know me?"

John pointed dumbly at the Guardian's forehead. "You've lost your crown," he said thickly.

The Guardian raised a hand to his brow. "The sea has claimed it, as it has claimed my land. It belongs to the Lyonesse: let it remain there. No longer have I the right to wear it, for I am now lord of nothing but a watery waste."

The Lord Trevelyan gazed into John's face. "It is not given to every man to see what manner of men shall follow him and bear his name. I have seen, and I am well content, though a score of generations may lie between us. Son of my sons, what name have you?"

The boy swallowed and realised that his mouth was hanging open. "John," he said quietly.

Trevelyan repeated the name, using a curious pronunciation which made it sound like 'Ewan'. "A good name . . . a Christian name." An earnest look came into his face. "You see, John, I could not have let you die. My horse is of no ordinary stock and is more fleet than any in Lyonesse, Belerion, Kernyw or the whole of Dumnonia. I knew that I could reach you in time, though I grew afraid when I lost sight of you and had to turn back. It was that which turned it into such a desperate race."

He stood up, flexing his legs. "I will not linger. I must turn my back on what has been and look to whatever may lie ahead. Will you ride with me again, my son? I have far to go, I think, but I will at least bring you safely to the circles of Bartinn."

SUNLIGHT was beginning to stream through the breaking clouds as ancestor and descendant rode calmly into the weird enclosure on the high summit of Bartinnê Hill. The bards, seated patiently on the surrounding bank, leapt to their feet as the horner blasted great notes of triumph into the air. Beside the trio of fires in the centre stood the silent, pensive figure of the Grand Bard, and both Corantyn and the beaming Gawen sprang forward to greet the boy as he swung down from Trevelyan's horse.

"Brave lad! Bravely done!" bellowed the dwarf, clapping him violently on the back, while Corantyn wrung his hand in greeting and relief. The elf led John forward, his silvery voice raised to address the assembly. "Bards of the Gorseth of Cornwall! The son of the lords returns from the flood. Behold the sword Dagrenou, Sword of Tears; the blade of Tristan the Sorrowful who was once among your number!"

A great shout went up, and arms were flung skyward in jubilation. The splendid figure of the Grand Bard, in his robes of deep blue and gold, stepped forward to place a gnarled hand on John's head. The grey eyes gazed into the boy's upturned face and the stern mouth softened into a smile.

"A perilous quest, John Trevelyan, and bravely fulfilled. Do you unsheath the Sword of Tears and lay it in my hands."

John drew the sword and handed it, hilt-first, to the old man who turned away and held it aloft.The sunlight caught its jewelled hilt and it flamed like a great torch.

The old man's voice called powerfully: "I charge the Powers of Light, of sun and moon and stars; of air and fire; of earth and water; of the west wind and the south wind and of the four seasons. Lay blessings upon this blade, and upon those who shall wield it in the name of the Light against the might of the Shadow!"

He stood with the sword held high, then lowered it to pass the blade slowly through the flames of each of the three fires, which glowed with an intense blue light with the passage of the sword.

The Grand Bard handed it back to John who took it gingerly, expecting it to be hot, but the sword was as cold as ice."It is not written whose hand shall wield it at the last," said the old man, "but if it be yours, use it well." He looked up. "My Lord Trevelyan, I would speak with you."

Trevelyan strode forward and checked, peering into the old man's face. "You!" he breathed incredulously. "But you are dead these fifteen years!"

The old man smiled tiredly. "I am not yet a phantom, old friend, but my time is close at hand. We who have lived by enchantment shall, at the last, fall by enchantment. The witch will yet ensnare me, for such is my destiny."

Trevelyan's eyes were cloudy. "A destiny was written for my country. To my eternal grief, I have seen it fulfilled."

"I too grieve for your country, Trevelyan, but through its fate shall rise much good. Arthur is avenged, but more importantly, his followers, the new bearers of his Light, are spared. Theirs is a new beginning; nigh thirty miles of ocean protects them from the Dark. I will tell you this: from that beginning, a great good will one day arise from the islands of Syllan, and the world will rejoice. But enough of such matters. Let us speak of the present: what think you of your descendant?"

"With pride have I witnessed his courage. If such is the manner of my children, and my children's children, then I shall live to my life's end with a joy known to no other."

"And where shall you go, now that you have no homeland?"

"To the court of Constantine, King of Dumnonia. He is not Arthur, but a good and just man nonetheless. I will tell him of this day . . . though not this part of it," he added thoughtfully. "He may find it in him to grant me lands. If so, I shall settle, take me a wife and begin the long chain which links me to this lad."

"Then may God speed you, Trevelyan. But hearken: speak not of me. My path through this world is at its end."

Trevelyan bowed briefly to the old man and turned to embrace John before remounting his horse. He gazed down at his young descendant for the last time. "Son of my sons," he said, "may the Powers of Light shine forever on you and your kin. Remember me, as I shall remember you."

He turned to ride away, the founder of a family on the white steed which would forever be their symbol. He looked back once, raising his hand in farewell, then, as he passed through the entrance of the ancient enclosure, his form shimmered like a mirage, faded and was gone.

John gazed at the spot where his ancestor had vanished and knew that Trevelyan had passed back to his own life, his own true time. He no longer had a part to play in this weird mingling of worlds. His own lay fifteen centuries away.

Corantyn moved to John's side. "Come," he said gently. "You have seen the past, but our purpose lies before us. Dry yourself by the Bardic fires before we prepare for the ride to Chysauster. The sun is westering."

"But my horse – ?

"She is here, and safe. She sensed disaster and in fear, fled back to us here. Do not blame her. I held no fears for you; the prophecy does not tell of your death."

"I don't remember it saying I'd survive, either," John retorted

"WE must reach Chysauster by sunset," said Corantyn as he, Gawen and John rode away from Bartinnê. "That is a village of this age and before this age, it still exists in our own time, where it is a curio for men to explore and wonder at. You shall see it as it was."

"Corantyn," said John, "the Grand Bard – Trevelyan knew him. So did you. I'm right, aren't I?"

Corantyn sighed. "I knew him, long ago. He was a great man. He came today as the Grand Bard of Cornwall but he was more than that. He was the Grand Bard of the Island of Britain; respected and revered by all. Yes, I knew him, as you also know him. He knew the Belerion prophecy better than any man alive or dead, for it was his own."

John stared into the distance. What Corantyn said was true; he had known the Grand Bard since his early childhood and, as he recalled, he had seen his face before. He had seen it twice, in fact: once in the tortured sky above the wreckage of the Lyonesse, and once as a carving on the cold granite of an ancient, candlelit tomb.

18: THE HOUSE OF SYLVESTRE

THE village of Chysauster hadn't been easy to spot until they drew close. The dozen low stone houses blended well into the hill-side and were remarkably similar to many John had seen in the lost land. The village was surrounded by acres of tiny fields, stone-hedged and terraced into the slope. Colourfully clad people at work in the fields looked at them curiously as the unlikely trio of riders approached.

They dismounted in front of a large house on the upper side of the winding track that passed for a village street. A heavy door opened and a vast man in his late fifties stepped out, flinging his arms wide in greeting.

His voice matched his build as he roared, "Welcome, my friends! Welcome to the house of Sylvestre!"

Corantyn stepped forward, grasping the massive forearm, "Well met, old friend. The years treat you kindly."

"They haven't done you so badly: not that it's easy to tell with you people of the Coraneid."

"Perhaps you are right," Corantyn replied, a little mischievously. "Since we last met, fifteen centuries have passed." His slanted eyebrows raised slightly at the chieftain's frown of puzzlement. "No, Sylvestre, I have not gone mad. What you see is the fulfilment of the prophecy."

"Welcome to the House of Sylvestre!"

Sylvestre's brow furrowed even further. "Ah," he said at last, "I begin to understand. 'Shall Times Intermingle' – am I right?" Corantyn nodded as the chieftain examined John from top to toe. "And your strangely clad young companion?"

"Is the son of the Lords. He is John, descendant of the Lord Trevelyan. He carries the sword Dagrenou, having borne it from the flood which has overwhelmed the Lyonesse."

Sadness clouded the chieftain's face. "Of that I know, for it was seen from the hill-tops. Is it the tinner you seek? He was here ere noon, and told of much strangeness before he left."

"He is not here now?"

"He rode eastward. You know his way; he comes and goes as he pleases, but seldom have I seen such purpose as there was in him. But why talk here when the home of Sylvestre awaits? Come, rest and be refreshed. Then we shall talk."

The house was oval in shape and the entrance passage led into an open courtyard. A large dog, lazing on the rough paving, growled softly at the newcomers until silenced by his master's command. To their left was a small room and a long, lean-to stable from whose shade the backside of a pale dun pony protruded, its long, shaggy tail swishing endlessly at flies. On the right, three doors led to rooms built into the great thickness of the surrounding wall.

Directly in front was the entrance to a round, thatched room into the dimness of which they were ushered by their host. There were no windows and a single pole, bedded in a socketed slab in the middle of the floor, rose high into the apex of the roof, and was lost in darkness. The warm day made the room almost unbearable and the door stood open to let in the cooler breezes of evening.

John sat with his back against the wall and looked round the room. Corantyn and Gawen were deep in conversation with Sylvestre, and a dark, wide-eyed girl sat as far away from the elf as she could. From the alarm she had shown when Corantyn entered the room, it was obvious that Sylvestre's granddaughter had never before encountered one of his race, other than in the scary pictures painted by old wives' tales. Despite assurances from her grandfather, and Corantyn's pleasant manner, the girl

Lowena's fears were not calmed. As for John's clothing, she had deduced it to be the work of magicians and witches, and she kept her distance from him as well.

Sylvestre listened to the tale, his face becoming grimmer. "And your final task is to breach the walls of Chûn ere midnight?" he said, shaking his head. "Need I remind you that many have tried and all have failed. Few have lived to tell the tale. It is madness. Where are your forces? What can three of you achieve without warriors, and you will need many. I have fifty men in the garrison on the hill above the village, but without a warlord –

"For such a task, you will need a special type of man; one who is proven in command and the strategy of battle. There is no such here. I am not a warrior, but a farmer – and do not remind me that even at my age I am still champion of the wrestlers of Belerion. I am both old and fat. Where is the horse that can bear me? Yet, in my younger days . . . " For a moment he was lost in nostalgia, but he pulled himself back from the past and looked up sharply.

"My friends, I am ashamed. I have allowed my guests to talk, with nothing to wet their throats. Lowena, do you fetch wine from the storeroom. Not that Gaulish pap. The best Mediterranean wine!"

The girl left the room while they gathered their thoughts. It seemed hopeless. With midnight barely four hours away, they were no further forward, even with the sword of Tristan in their possession. John stared miserably at his feet. He couldn't even contact Ben; he waited fifteen centuries away.

A sudden commotion outside roused him from his private misery. The dog was barking loudly, drowning Lowena's shouts for her grandfather. Sylvestre hauled himself to his feet, bawling at the dog which slunk off into a corner.

"Grandfather! Riders are coming! A war-host! Come quickly!"

"Raiders!" cried the chieftain, lumbering from the house and shouting to rouse the villagers. "Arm yourselves! Put all women and children in the houses. Lowena, get yourself inside and bar the doors. Why was no beacon lit? Are they asleep in the fortress?"

Gawen drew his axe and hurried outside, with John and Corantyn at his heels. The elf had an arrow at the ready and he dropped to one knee to aim his longbow. John hung back, closer to the door of the house, but his fingers curled tightly around the hilt of the Sword of Tears.

To the north-east, a trackway ran down the hill-side to the outskirts of the village, and lingering clouds of dust hung over it. A thunder of hoofs thrummed in the air and the dying sunlight glinted sharply from mail and spearhead.

There was pandemonium in the village. Men hardly trained or dressed for combat rushed out of houses and fields clutching axes and scythes, while children and women, some carrying bawling infants, dashed indoors. Finally a pathetic line of twenty or so farmers stood alongside Sylvestre and his guests.

"What chance have we?" the chieftain muttered. "Look at them: a hundred and more. Warriors all." His brows knotted in question. "But these are not Saxons or pirates from Eriu. These are mounted men – British Celts! Our own kind!" He reddened in fury. "What cowardly renegade would lead such a raid on his own people!"

But John was leaping up and down in excitement, his eyes fixed on the leader of the war-party. Surely there could only be one man of such size and stature. "Rialobran!" he yelled.

Corantyn breathed in sharply, lowering his bow. "In truth, it is the son of Cunoval!"

"Arthur's beard, so it is!" Sylvestre's fury turned instantly to delight. "Lower your arms, my people," he yelled above the din.

"No other mortal man has the equal of his stature," said Corantyn, "and no horse in the world is the match of Taranwyn. See, the Duke Selus rides with him, and the sons of Gyfyan, so many faces I remember. And there – there is our very own Jack of the Hammer! Ah, Sylvestre! Here is our war-host and our battle-chief, and hope rides with them!"

The war-band entered the village in a welter of hoofbeats and ringing cries of greeting. John ran to meet the tinner. "Jack! So your guess was right!"

The tinner grinned at him. "And Rialobran has been busy since he rose from his stone. Look at the warriors he has called to his side. They gathered at the fort on the Hayle, and I met them on the road."

"How many?" Gawen cut in impatiently.

"Two hundred," the tinner replied, "and more wait at Bosprenis, Porthmeor and Bodinnar. We will be three hundred in all."

"And fifty of my own," pledged Sylvestre. "But how many serve Pengersek?"

The tinner's face darkened. "I sent birds to spy out the land. Word came back that he has called the spriggans of Trencrom, Kenidjack and all their warrens. A thousand goblins guard Chûn Castle and they were never cowards for all their skulking in mists and dark places. Remember, too, the Nôshelyas, the seven hunters of the night who cannot be slain by earthly means.

"Worse, we have not the strength of surprise. Only a handful of birds came back from Chûn, and those in poor shape. No, my friends, we are expected."

John stared at him in horror. "Three hundred and fifty against a thousand? It's not enough. We need more men."

A white horse moved beside him, whose size was breathtaking. She stood more than twenty hands high, a massive creature who rippled with muscle; her like has not been seen in the world for many a long century. Over her face was a war-mask of bronze, beautifully worked and fitted at the forehead with a long, vicious horn. She had been well named Taranwyn, White Thunder.

Her rider was no less awesome. Rialobran, Prince of sixth century Belerion, was a giant; scarcely less than eight feet tall. Helmetless, wild-haired and keen-eyed, his bare arms were thickly muscled and bore the scars of a hundred conflicts. He wore a battle-coat of bronze plates and his cloak was of royal purple. A sweeping moustache almost hid the stern mouth, and his eyes glittered coldly at John's despair.

"Your words, boy, spring from neither heart nor head," he said. "Are you truly so ignorant of Celtic valour? Then hearken well. At Mount Badon the forces of Arthur, a thousand strong, faced three times that number of Saxons yet won a famous victory. Night approaches and we ride for Chûn. Do you stay, prattling with fear, or do you ride with us?"

"Nay, Prince," said Corantyn. "You judge him harshly. This is the descendant of Trevelyan, whose courage has delivered the blade of Tristan from the flood."

The giant stared curiously at the boy. Stung by his words, John glared back, defiantly. The Prince shouted suddenly, laughter in his voice.

"Lo, my warriors! See how he defies me! How many would so dare? The elf-lord speaks truly; the lad has courage indeed. Son of Trevelyan, I crave pardon for hasty words. Do you ride beside me, here at my right hand. Together we shall drive the conjurer and all his minions into the Pit itself!"

19: GOLOWAN EVE

THE hill of Watch Croft, as it is called in our own time, is the highest point of the Penwith range and its ancient name has been lost to memory. It is bleak and bare, windswept and boulder-studed, with black knobs of jointed granite jutting from dwarf gorse and heather.

The warriors waited on the hill-top, watching the moon climb high into the night sky. John shifted uneasily in his saddle and glanced round at the silent horsemen: the two hundred brought by Rialobran; Sylvestre's fifty; and a further fifty gathered from the villages of Bosprenis and Porthmeor.

On the top of the hill, a man-sized standing stone guarded a great cairn which had once been raised over the ashes of a long-forgotten king. John watched, enthralled, as the giant prince dismounted and stood before the barrow with drawn sword to salute the memory of the unknown monarch.

Rialobran turned away, pointing with the naked blade to the south-west. "The moon shows us our goal," he said tersely. A mile or more away the grim walls of Chûn Castle stood white and starkly shadowed on their hill. "The question," mused the prince, "is how to breach those walls." Then, glancing at Jack, "You built the castle well, friend tinner. Perhaps too well."

The tinner's face was grim. "I built it to protect my own," he said in a dangerously quiet voice, "not to provide a haven for warlocks and trolls."

The prince frowned. "You find offence where none was intended."

Jack smiled thinly. "No words of yours could offend me, prince. It is the fouling of my ancient home that irks me."

"Then who knows," said Rialobran, "perhaps the hand that built it will be that which destroys it!"

Jack made no reply and the prince turned to his commanders. "Sons of Gyfyan, now is the time! Ride south and swiftly to Bodinnar where further warriors await. From there, take the old way flanking the west side of Dry Carn to where it meets the ridgeway track on The Gump. Your assault on the castle will be from the ridgeway, on its southern side."

The twin brothers, Sulyan and Gwythno, swung away to ride down the hill-side and became lost in the darkness. The waiting seemed endless and, with Rialobran closely watching the passage of the moon, scarcely a word was spoken. After a while, the prince called Corantyn, Selus and other officers to him and they conversed intensely for a while. Heads nodded and shook, hands and arms gestured until, at last, Selus came away to remount his horse. With a brief salute to his prince, and with a hundred men behind him, he began the descent of the steep northern face of the hill towards the sea.

"The strategy seems sound enough," commented Jack, half to himself. He caught John looking blankly at him and explained. "The Duke Selus descends to the cliff-top track where he will travel westward. At the well of Morveth, he will turn inland, up the valley to Crofto to approach Chûn from the north. In the meantime, the sons of Gyfyan, who have further to ride, will make their attack from the south-west, while we attack from the north-east. If I am right, we must wait a little longer so that our three forces will make their onslaught together, from three sides."

"But surely the timing's sheer guesswork," said John. "What happens if we don't all get there at the same time?"

"What a one you are for black thoughts! But there are advantages even there; as the enemy concentrates on the first attack, weak spots will appear for the others to exploit when they arrive. Even so," he added, "it will go hard for whoever gets there first. That most likely will be us."

Their attention was drawn away by the voice of Rialobran, who sat once more on his warhorse. His sword pointed at the southern sky.

"When the cloud masks the moon, then shall we ride!"

To John, the cloud and the moon seemed miles from each other, but they met in a surprisingly short time. The night darkened and, through the darkness, came the voice of the prince, terrible in its calmness.

"Now, my warriors. A castle to take and its contents to trample!"

AT the base of Chûn's rounded hill, and straddling the ancient trackway, lay a village much like Chysauster, but it had long been abandoned, its walls overgrown and decaying, its roof collapsed. Its name was Bosullow Trehyllys.

Corantyn's watchful eyes narrowed as the silent ruins came into view, and the edges of his nostrils flared slightly.

"Have a care. We are not alone."

Rialobran reined in. "What say you, elf-lord?"

"Bosullow hides goblins."

"Ambush?" John said uneasily.

"So they intend." Jack of the Hammer wore a carefree smile. "But it is we who have surprise on our side. The eyes of Corantyn are sharp, especially in the night, but it seems his nose is sharper. The fault lies with the spriggans themselves; they should wash occasionally."

"You treat this lightly," said Rialobran testily. "They force us to storm the village, wasting time we can ill afford."

"Then why waste it?" The tinner laughed softly. "Sit your horse, prince, and watch the fun at your leisure."

He drew the ironstone charm from his neck, held it by its leather thong and began to swing it round his head. "Corantyn. Where are they?"

The elf pointed. "Fifty paces," he said.

Jack stood high in his stirrups, still swinging the ironstone.

Faster and faster it whirled, then, suddenly, he released it. Glittering in the moonlight, and with its thong streaming out behind it like a tail, the ironstone sailed in a graceful arc into the very heart of the ruined village.

A brief flash erupted, and a thin, bubbling scream rose and fell. Harsh voices raised a babble of confusion and wraith-like shapes scattered in panic, fleeing into the night.

"Ha!" barked Rialobran, "your bite is a deep one, tinner. So our path lies clear."

Jack turned his horse aside.

"Where do you go?" called Corantyn.

"To recover my ironstone."

"You will never find it in all that bracken, and in darkness. Leave it, there is no time to look for it now."

The tinner scowled at the shadowy ruins. "So be it, elf-lord," he said with reluctance. "But we shall have cause to rue its loss."

The trackway opened into the moor and before them rose the hill; an unbroken slope to the great walls of Chûn. A mighty shout, the war-cry of the Prince of Belerion, roared out and was echoed in a hundred throats. It was the signal to charge.

The reality of his position suddenly came home to John. Fear clutched at the pit of his stomach in the knowledge that the only way now was forward, into the nightmare of battle.

The company split into three. To the right went a division led by a burly man with a scarred face. His name, John remembered, was Gorheder. To the left went Jack of the Hammer, with more warriors, while up the hill, making straight for the castle, thundered the main force: Rialobran at the head, Corantyn, Gawen and John behind, and warriors on either hand, spreading into a line with glittering spearheads lowered in readiness.

Out of the bracken rose a hundred howling goblins, hurling volleys of slingshot. Palefaced but alert, John ducked low over his pony's neck as the air thickened with the lethal hail of fist-sized pebbles.

Rialobran contemptuously ignored the missiles – John saw two stones crash into the giant's chest, with no apparent effect – and spurred his great horse toward the enemy lines. A man-sized goblin, even more hideous and ill-favoured than most of his kind, leapt into his path, menacingly swinging a huge axe of greenstone.

The mare Taranwyn lowered her head. John shut his eyes at the moment of impact, but the sound of the collision came clearly to his ears. When he looked again, he saw the spriggan horribly impaled on the horn of the mare's war-mask, dead fingers still clutching the axe. The horse tossed her head, almost with contempt, hurling the goblin's broken body into the midst of his fellows.

That the spriggan had been of high rank was evident from the wail of dismay that went up. Momentary confusion set in, and the warriors, sensing the brief advantage, hurled themselves into the fight.

A stone whined past John's ear from behind, where a further host of goblins had risen from well-planned concealment, catching them in vicious crossfire. He heard the gruff voice of Gawen cry out: "They have cut off our retreat!"

Rialobran, casting away his broken, bloody spear and drawing his bright sword, twisted in the saddle, roaring: "Our way is forward, not back!"

"But where are Selus and the others?" shouted John. "They should be here by now!"

BEN Trevelyan turned the television off and settled wearily back in his armchair. The stillness of the room was oppressive and his thoughts lay somewhere on the moor where his nephew and niece were in deep trouble. But where? There had been no word of their movements, their plans, nothing. His belated trip to the Mên-an-Tol had been fruitless: not a soul had stirred for miles around, and only the wind had given reply to his frantic calls. Worry and a feeling of utter helplessness gnawed at him and he wished that he hadn't shooed the Hoskens away to their beds.

He looked round the room, searching for something, anything, to occupy his mind; something that might offer a clue or inspiration. He settled for watching the dwindling dot on the television screen and gazed vacantly at it as it slowly shrank.

He sat up with a jerk, hands gripping the arms of the chair with bloodless knuckles. The dot wasn't shrinking . . . it was growing!

Wider and wider it grew, until the screen was alive with light. A picture began to form, and sounds started to emerge: metallic clashes, cries, shouts, the drumming of horses' hoofs.

The picture leapt into focus. It was a battle; a bloody conflict with no quarter sought or given. Wild-haired horsemen, cloaked and mailed, swung their swords in savage arcs against ugly, misshapen creatures like gargoyles, grey of skin and cat-eyed, wielding slings, axes and long stone knives.

A smaller figure, mounted on a chestnut pony, came into view. He was wildly swinging a sword, as large as himself, with a jewelled hilt that glittered and flashed in the moonlight. It was John. Grotesque, hairless creatures fell to the bite of the sword as John urged the pony further into the fray. The boy battled furiously, his eyes wild, until the pony, maddened with fear, reared and flung its rider headlong into the mass of struggling bodies.

Ben leapt to his feet with a cry, but the boy was quickly shielded by two familiar figures: one, a tall elf; the other, a bearded dwarf who swung a double-bladed axe with terrible effect. The elf calmly raised his great longbow and a slim shaft whined away, accurate and deadly.

The boy jumped to his feet and, in the same movement, flung himself forward to cut down a goblin poised to strike at the elf's unprotected back.

The scene changed, but the clash of battle could still be distantly heard as Ben saw a lordly figure, robed in black silk, hands upraised to draw power to his spells; the man he knew as the mysterious eccentric called Henry Milliton. And yet this man was as far removed from the enigmatic figure of Milliton as he himself was from a tramp.

The field of vision grew wider and Ben could see that the Witch-Lord stood on a great slab of unhewn stone while at his feet lay a still form sheathed in robes of the purest white, which glowed in the light of the full moon. Her eyes were closed, her face peaceful, and only the soft rise and fall of her breast showed that she still lived. And there on her breast lay the Crownstone. Its facets seemed to wink at him, and he knew at that moment that its power had reached out to call him.

Hope surged through him. Both John and Penny were alive, if in deadly danger, but he also had the certainty that he knew where they were. He had only needed the slightest clue, and the Crownstone had given him that. He threw on his jacket, and as he did so, the battle-sounds ceased and the screen went blank. The door slammed shut behind him and, on the wall of the empty room, the hands of the clock crawled relentlessly on towards midnight.

20: THE GATES OF CHÛN

THE battle raged furiously as John, now on foot and with Gawen and Corantyn beside him, pressed on towards the walls of the castle, driving a blood-soaked path through the rank smelling mob that milled around them.

It might have been instinct that made John glance round, just in time to glimpse a large and particularly repulsive goblin rising from the pack. A bony arm swung and an object flew through the air towards him. John leapt aside, knocking Gawen to the ground in his haste, but even so he was not quite quick enough and the missile crashed agonisingly into the back of his shoulder. Half stunned by the impact, he fell to his knees.

Luck was with him. The greenstone axe had struck him obliquely, glancing off, but he felt the warm stickiness of fresh blood. Strong hands hauled him to his feet and hurried fingers, none too gentle, parted the torn cloth of his sweatshirt.

"Fortune smiles on you," said Gawen. "If the axe had struck as intended, you would surely have no arm. But the cut is small; it will not slay you."

A curious surge of strength and courage swept through the boy. "Only a scratch?" he muttered. "Let's go on, Gawen, I'm ready." The dwarf's teeth glinted in the moonlight and he moved like lightning to sink his axe into yet another pale, deceptively wasted body.

The bow of Corantyn sent death with every shaft, but even he had not gone unscathed. A cut forearm trickled blood and as John caught sight of it he drew his breath, for the elf's blood was thin, pale and weak.

"Aye," said Gawen softly, taking advantage of a momentary lull in the fighting. "There you see for yourself the weakness of the elves. The will is strong, but the blood – it lacks the strength to resist the new poisons which men are spreading across the world. Many of his people have died, and many more will die. He himself has sickened more than once, but the arts of the tinner are many, and so he lives."

Corantyn looked round and even his normally tranquil face was drawn. There seemed to be no end of the spriggans who were beginning to press them back. A mounted warrior, crazily chanting his death song, was swept from his horse by a swarm of bony hands and overwhelmed. His sword flickered briefly and was lost from sight.

"We need to find new strength if we are to have any hopes of winning this field," said the elf.

"And so we shall, my friends." Jack of the Hammer, also on foot, appeared from the mêlée. He raised his awesome hammer which glinted redly.

Gawen bellowed a roar of defiance. Axe, hammer, bow and the glittering Sword of Tears rose in anger. The nearest goblins checked, momentarily uncertain, and their hesitation spurred the four on. The tinner's impenetrable bull's hide coat rang under the assault of greenstone blades and maces, and the jewels of the sword from Lyonesse caught the moonlight, sketching patterns in the night air. A dozen goblins fell before their onslaught but it seemed that as each fell, three more were there to take its place. John's strength began to falter and, as he desperately parried a thrust from a barbed spear, he staggered and fell.

Jack caught him under the arms, dragging him backwards. "Back!" he cried. "Back! They are too many!"

Goblins moved in behind them, cutting off their route of escape, and suddenly there was no place to go. Grinning, triumphant faces pressed in from all sides, their weapons raised for the final slaughter.

Out of the night came the Prince of Belerion. His great warhorse thundered over the ground and his mighty sword lashed out to left and right. Goblins fell, hissing and screeching, before the onslaught of the giant, and their way lay open for escape.

At the same time, a loud cry cut through the night and the drumming of galloping horses shook the ground. John's sobbing breath rushed out in relief as, up the hill-side from the south-west, raced the identical skewbald steeds of the twin sons of Gyfyan with fifty men in their wake. The battle grew fiercer and louder and another shout, from a hundred more throats, went up from the far side of the castle. Selus and his force had arrived.

The spriggans fell back to the castle gates. Slingshot and spears rained from the massive walls but the Celts, prouds and merciless, pressed relentlessly forward.

"Nôshelyas!" came an urgent cry. "The hunters! The hunters!"

Struggling against fatigue, John saw that the heavy outer gate of the hill fort lay open and six horsemen, with hoods and robes of shadows, streamed out. The eyes of their black horses rolled with the terror of the creatures on their backs. The six checked for a second, their hooded, glowing eyes taking stock of the battle, then, uttering terrible cries, they hurled themselves into the fight.

John glanced about the hill-side for any possible surprise assault but there was nothing to be seen. He paused, frowning. Something was wrong, he knew it; he could not ignore the alarm bells of his mind. But what? The question gnawed at him, but there was no time to dwell on it. He twisted his head again to watch the Night Hunters as they raced into battle against the forces of Selus and the sons of Gyfyan. Again his brows lowered in question. "Six?" he wondered. "So where's the seventh?"

BEN drove through the night like a madman. He had taken more than one corner on two wheels and the Land Rover swayed alarmingly as the farmer forced it on at breakneck speed, praying that any roving police cars were patrolling other roads. He swerved violently to avoid a wayward fox as he shot past the little Land's End airport, and all but overturned. Up onto the grass verge he went, fighting to control the crazily bucking vehicle and to turn it back onto the road. Down into the Cot Valley he charged, and up the steep, twisting hill on the far side. Then, he cursed

Near the top of the hill, like a solid wall across the road, lay a dense bank of white fog. Ben swore violently, forced to cut his speed as he entered it. The engine faltered, spluttered and died. His hand flew to the ignition key, turning it once, twice, three times. There was no response.

Thick silence pressed in on him; his head reeled and as quickly cleared again. He stared out through the windscreen in utter amazement.

The mist had vanished . . . but so had the road. The Land Rover stood on scrubby moorland. The houses which should have been standing nearby had gone. Ben knew he'd reached the outskirts of St Just, but the town wasn't there. The familiar field pattern had, for the most part, disappeared and those fields that remained were unfamiliar.

Bright moonlight shone on a new, alien landscape. Before him lay thickly wooded valleys and beyond them rose a hill, twin-peaked and barren. Ben fixed his gaze on the hill-top beyond the valley, and on the stark outcrop of granite crowning the right hand peak.

He smiled grimly. What had happened was far beyond his comprehension, but he realised that whatever strangeness had changed the lanscape had not altered the appearance of Carn Kenidjack. There weren't two places like that in the world. Beyond the tell-tale crag was a crimson glow in the sky. Ben stared at it for a moment, then turned on the ignition.

He wasn't in the least surprised when the engine burst straight into life.

JACK of the Hammer snatched an arrow from Corantyn's quiver and began to wrap handfuls of dry bracken around its slender shaft. The elf watched him quizzically.

"Long ago," said Jack, without looking up from his work,

"before even you walked the earth, I built this fortress to house and protect my family, and to guard the trade in tin. Who better to know its only weakness? – The buildings which stand against the back of the inner wall are roofed with dry thatch and, if the spriggans fear anything, it is naked flame, so let us ring those inside with fire."

Corantyn wasted no time, but bent to join the tinner in his work. Finally, he nocked an arrow to the bowstring and Jack's tinderbox provided the flame. The great bow sang.

Startled eyes looked up as the fiery missile arched high over the walls of the fortress, closely followed by a second. John's heart leapt into his mouth and he yelled desperately: "No, you idiots! Penny's in there!"

"Be still, John," said the tinner calmly. "She will not be harmed. There is a large open courtyard in the centre of the castle. It will be safe for her there but, with luck, the spriggans may be forced out for they have a mortal dread of fire. We have to break into the castle by midnight and we will not do that by battering our heads against its walls. Have no fears for your sister's safety, John, she is protected by the Crownstone. Pengersek will not risk harm to either her or the Stone. Not at this stage, so close to the witching hour."

A glow appeared above the castle walls and a flame licked upwards. Another writhed up beside it, and a third. Soon a curtain of fire roared above the battlements. Screams of pain and panic rang out from within and the Celtic warriors raised a ragged cheer.

The massive gates crashed open for a second time and scores of goblins, crazed with fear, poured out of the burning fortress. Many were themselves ablaze, screaming horribly and flapping uselessly at the flames before collapsing and writhing feebly on the ground. But there was no sign of either Pengersek or Penny.

The unscathed spriggans lent their weight to the battle, but the heavily outnumbered Celts fought grimly on, somehow holding their ground. The six Night Hunters, ambassadors of evil, wielded their swords of jet with terrifying venom, slashing and hewing. Any sword which pierced their robes and there were many, found nothing beneath on which to bite, and their iron blades smouldered and crumbled away. With each life they took, the shadowed eyes beneath the deep cowls burned ever brighter, and none could withstand their onslaught.

Corantyn bent his bow, sending an arrow true to the heart of the nearest hunter, but willow and flint fared no better than iron. The demon laughed coldly, spurring his horse on. The elf's uncanny swiftness was the saving of him as the dark blade swept down, slicing the air where his head had been the blink of an eye before. A severed lock of silver-gold hair floated to the ground. The black horse was cruelly turned about and the black sword swung up for a second strike.

John raced forward, shouting at the top of his voice and the sword of Tristan suddenly blazed bright in his hand. The demon stiffened abruptly, wheeled his horse, and was gone. Corantyn climbed to his feet, gazing in wonder at the jewelled sword whose unearthly light had again grown dim.

"Could it be – ?" he began, but other eyes had seen; another mind was quicker. Immense hoofs crashed into the turf beside them and an urgent voice rang out: "The sword, boy! Give me Tristan's sword!"

John looked up dumbly. The heaving, foaming flanks of the horse Taranwyn towered over him and the hand of her giant rider stretched out impatiently. The boy lifted the sword, offering it hilt-first. Rialobrán took it and raised the gem-studded hilt to his lips.

"So that is it!" he breathed. "Sky-iron! Now I understand why you were sent into the Lyonesse!" He looked down at the boy. "And now you are weaponless." He unbuckled his own huge sword. "Here is my own blade, which is named Gwythyas Howlsedhas: Guardian of the West. I charge it to your keeping, young warrior. Keep it well, for the works of Merlin foretell of a day when Belerion will again face danger. On that day, which lies within your own time, a man will come to claim it in my name. Until then, son of Trevelyan, it will serve you as it has served me; I know you have the strength to wield it. Take it!" he urged as John hesitated. "I no longer have need of it."

John staggered under the weight of the massive sword as Rialobran turned his warhorse towards the burning gate of the castle. The clamour and confusion faltered and died, weapons halted in mid-stroke, and all eyes were drawn to the wild prince and to Dagrenou, Sword of Tears, for, as he raised it to the sky, so it blazed with a great light and flames of the palest blue flowed along its blade. Eyes narrowed against its glare as Rialobran halted before the burning gates of Chûn.

For a moment, all was still and a deathly hush, broken only by the relentless roar of the flames, fell upon the hill. Then, behind the wall of fire, a shape moved, and through the gate, slowly and deliberately, oblivious to the blaze and collapsing masonry, rode the captain of the Night Hunters. John caught his breath as he watched horse and rider walk calmly through the raging fire, unharmed and unafraid.

"That is surely no horse," growled Gawen softly. "See its eyes; how they burn. It is Pengersek's mare, a devil in horse-shape. Demon rides upon demon!" The boy gave a start: "Daemon rides daemon." Another prophetic line had come true.

On came the devil-horse and its ghastly rider. The mare was as black as midnight, save only a white, diamond-shaped star in the centre of her forehead. Her baleful eyes glittered disdainfully and the breath from the flared nostrils smoked like a smouldering fire.

They halted some yards from the waiting figure of Rialobran. Taranwyn's ears flattened to her skull and she lowered her head menacingly. A massive, iron-shod hoof pawed the ground.

For a long, silent minute, demon and prince faced each other, then the gloved hands of the hunter reached up to draw back his hood and reveal the face no earthly eyes had ever seen. A gasp rose from every throat.

It was the face of an angel: beautiful, majestic, magnificent. But it was an angel of darkness, for the cold eyes glittered with evil and nothing could conceal the short horns raking forward from the golden-curled temples, their sharp points tipped with gleaming metal.

The vision lasted no more than an instant as the black sword hissed from its sheath and the demon's mouth twisted and snarled with fury.

The sword from the Lyonesse flashed once more as Rialobran tossed it high into the air, and it traced a glowing arc before being deftly caught by the prince's right hand. The demon's snarl was answered by a deafening battle-cry; the words of Celtic defiance echoing through the granite hills and into the night.

Black horse and white came together in a welter of pounding hoofs. Taranwyn's lowered head sought its target unerringly and the terrible bronze horn of her war-mask ripped open the flank of the demon-mare in a ghastly crimson gash. She staggered, twisting away and screaming with pain, then, to the horror of all who saw, the gaping wound closed, healing before their eyes as though it had never been.

The Hunter turned her again and his sword swept down onto the prince's shield as he whipped it up to protect his helmetless head. In the same movement, Rialobran aimed a vicious stroke in reply, but the demon was quicker, pulling back his weapon to block the shining blade. The clash rang out deafeningly and, as the Sword of Tears blazed yet again, the black blade of the Hunter shivered to fragments.

Rialobran slashed savagely back at the demon, using both hands to add power to the back-handed blow. The glowing blade left a path of light in its wake.

There was a brief, terrible vision of the horned head leaping from the sombre shoulders, followed by a dazzling flare of light, cries of eternal anguish, and a joyous shout of Celtic triumph. Then, darkness and silence fell like stones.

The Nôshelyas, all seven of them, had vanished and only their terrified steeds remained. There was no trace of Prince Rialobran or his magnificent mare, yet the ghostly image of a glowing sword hung, point downward, in the air for an instant before fading and vanishing for ever.

A wail of despair went up from the goblin hordes. Their commanders destroyed, they were lost. Dropping their weapons as one, and leaving their wounded to fend for themselves. they fled, scattering into the night. John stood aghast, unable to speak, but Corantyn answered the question he could not voice.

"Peace, John. All is well with Prince Rialobran. He has fulfilled his task and at last he goes to take his long-awaited place in Enys Avallen; in the Halls of the Brave. He will not return, unless it be at Arthur's side when he comes again.

Black horse and white came together in a welter of pounding hoofs

"As for the Nôshelyas: it has long been written that the destruction of one would be the bane of them all. Their reign of terror is over and it was Dagrenou that sealed their fate. Made of sky-iron, it was sent by the Ultimate Power of Light. Nothing from the evil of the Shadowlands could withstand it."

John gazed down at the massive sword in his hands.

"That also is a fine sword," said the elf, "and one to be treasured. Do you see the words of the Roman tongue etched into the blade? They say: 'This is the blade of Rialobran of Belerion, son of Cunoval King. The Raven alone shall wield it, save he who is worthy'."

John hung his head. "Then I have no right to hold it."

"Not so." The elf shook his head. "He himself passed it into your care, for you have proved your worthiness."

"But this man who'll come for it – ?"

"I know not, John. That, I think, will be another story for which we must wait."

There was a curious coughing sound. John turned and beside him stood Gawen who wore a strange, surprised expression, wide-eyed and bewildered. The dwarf coughed again; a peculiar, rasping bark which shook his entire body, and a thin stream of blood dribbled into the beard from his half-open mouth. He lurched forward and John caught sight of the crude hilt of a stone knife between the dwarf's shoulder-blades, pinning his cloak to his back; the parting shot of a dying spriggan. The boy stood helplessly as Gawen's knees began to buckle under him.

"Hold me, lad!" he gasped. "Hold me up!"

John took his right arm, Corantyn the left, and together they bore the dwarf's weight.

"Thank you, my friends," he whispered. "It has always been my dream that when Death comes to claim me, I should stand, face him and be proud. I will not die on my back, but on my feet." The life in his eyes was fading fast and he coughed again, painfully. Again, blood ran from his mouth and he spat disdainfully. "I am content," he said, after taking a gulping breath, hungry for air. "I die the death of a warrior, and among no truer comrades. John?" The word came as though the dwarf had suddenly found himself alone. "Brave lad: when I am gone, lay me within the castle. Let me be taken by the flames; it is my wish. I cannot bear the thought of a barrow weighing me down." The dwarf's head slumped forward onto his ample chest and the body sagged heavily.

"Gawen!" John cried out, but the dwarf's eyes had glazed over, staring lifelessly at the ground.

"Gawen the warrior has left us," said Corantyn gently. "Help me to carry him. We must honour his dying wish."

They raised up the little warrior, to bear him through the smouldering gates and into the castle. Already it was filled with men, frantically searching for Pengersek, despite the intense heat and danger of the blaze. One of the buildings which lined the great inner wall remained unburned but it was only to be a matter of minutes before the hungry flames came to devour it.

They laid the body of Gawen in the smoke-filled chamber, wrapping his cloak around him and laying his trusty war-axe on his chest. Corantyn knelt to close the eyes. "Farewell, old friend," he murmured, then turned and strode wearily outside. John gazed silently with tear-filled eyes for a moment at the little corpse – there were no words he could find – then he too left the room.

Jack of the Hammer, pushing his way through the milling searchers, called out to them. His face, already strained, fell still further as he caught sight of the body within the open door of the building.

"A knife in the back," Corantyn explained. "But he was content at the last." He gestured up at the flames which were already beginning to lick at the thatched roof. "This was his final wish."

Jack tore his shocked gaze away. "The castle is empty; Pengersek and the girl are not here. Every corner has been searched; there were sorcerous trappings in the gatehouse, but that was all. We have fallen for a trick as old as time, and at what cost!" He looked again at the body of Gawen. "There can only be minutes left."

"But they must be here!" Even Corantyn's customary calmness was showing the strain. "The Mên-an-tol does not lie: it clearly pointed here, to Chûn Castle."

John turned away, devastated. After all this, the sorcerer's deceit had beaten them. All the anxiety, the fighting . . . Gawen . . . had all been for nothing. Wherever he was, Marek the Witch-Lord had won.

'Wherever he was?' the thought suddenly came to him. Had the holed stone deceived them? Was it inspiration, or just a straw to clutch at? He didn't know, but it was some sort of hope. Had he been the only person to have noticed that there had been something odd about the hill-side? He now knew what: the landscape had not been complete.

"No!" he shouted, "you're wrong! You're all wrong! The Mên-an-tol didn't lie. It wasn't pointing at Chûn Castle at all. It was pointing beyond it -to Chûn Quoit!" He turned and ran from the castle, Corantyn and Jack at his heels.

"Look!"

Beneath the cold rays of the full moon stood the primeval tomb of Chn Quoit, harbouring its eerie ritual, where, until now, it had lain hidden.

"So!" breathed Corantyn, "I begin to understand. The Witch-Lord used his arts to conceal himself while we wasted time storming the castle – and would he not have sealed such a spell into something he believed indestructible?"

"The Nôshelyas!" said Jack. "By all the tin on Iktis, the prince served us well!" He turned back to the hill fort, shouting for all he was worth, "Warriors! To horse! To horse!"

"Why would Pengersek choose a place like the Quoit for his ritual?" John puzzled.

Corantyn's face remained expressionless as he replied. "It is a place of the dead."

21: THE HOUR IS COME

MAREK, Lord of Pengersek, glanced up from his work as the horsemen thundered down the hill towards him. The flames of the burning ruin of Chûn Castle reflected from mail and sword, and the tips of spears were blazing points of fire. Alarm flashed briefly in his dark eyes but quickly passed as he noted the position of the moon. A smile touched the corners of his lips. His preparations were over; he had only to wait for midnight, just moments away.

Around the edge of the mound in which the Quoit stood was a circle of twelve monk-like figures, grey of cowl and habit, whose forms shimmered as though seen through the haze of summer heat.

The warriors rode onward to the ancient tomb. Its massive capstone glowed eerily in the moonlight and the dark figure which stood upon it was a statue of jet. At the sorcerer's feet lay the still form of Penny Trevelyan, her twentieth century clothing concealed by a rich gown of white samite, and her fair hair spilled onto the cold granite beneath her head. On her breast, and still attached to its golden chain, lay the Crownstone of Lyonesse, half-hidden by an eerie column of slowly twisting vapour, shot through with luminous colours, which issued from four curiously wrought vessels placed close to the girl's head.

The riders bore down on the cowled figures, which stood motionless and strangely unconcerned.

A harsh command rang out: "Ride them down!"

The warrior Gorheder, his scarred face set, spurred his horse on, straight at the nearest figure. His notched sword swept back for the kill, then a cry of alarm burst from John's lips.

Both horse and rider seemed to pass straight through the ghostly form as though it were made of mist. There was a sharp crack, the acrid stench of sulphur stung their nostrils, and both horse and warrior fell, smoking, to the ground and lay still. The monkish figure stood as silent and unmoving as before.

Corantyn reined in sharply, jerking upright in his saddle and flinging his hand into the air. "Hold! More witchcraft!"

"An astute observation," Pengersek smiled pleasantly and his voice was gently mocking. "Welcome. I welcome you all. You are privileged to witness this event. Uninvited, but welcome all the same."

"I will be privileged only to see your foul carcass feeding the ravens." It was the Duke Selus, hard-eyed and stern, who spoke.

Pengersek regarded the warrior with languid interest and spoke like a schoolmaster scolding a mischievous boy, his words heavy with sarcasm. "One so helpless . . . and, make no mistake, you are helpless . . . should mind his manners when addressing his betters."

"Betters!" spat the warrior.

"Peace, my friends," said Corantyn. "He seeks only to gain time."

"Of which, elf-lord, there is precious little," Pengersek reminded him. His eyes roved about the hostile faces. "Ah, now there is a face I recall: Jack of the Hammer," he said smoothly. "Long it is since we met. This time, I shall be the victor."

The Witch-Lord pondered briefly. "So this is the meaning of the Belerion prophecy. One of the Merlin's rantings, if my memory serves me well. 'Shall Times Intermingle.' I will admit to having been somewhat mystified by that line. However, you will agree that the verses are open-ended. They do not foretell the final victor, and all the time you have acted in the blind faith that it was you. How ironic!

"I take it that it was Tristan's blade, the Sword of Tears, which destroyed the Nôshelyas, and you brave people sent a snivelling boy into the Lyonesse to do the work you had no stomach to do yourselves." His eyes fell on John, who glared at him with hatred. "You did well, my boy. Brave work, indeed, but the sword has gone. It cannot help you now."

The Witch-Lord laughed at the torture in the boy's face. He gestured dramatically, sweeping first the left hand, then the right, in wide arcs, and the monk-like figures vanished.

"A barrier removed," he smiled. "But it helps you not. My sorcery and the magic of the Eve of Golowan is proof against you all."

His voice changed to an angrier tone. "Dare you believe that Marek of Pengersek can be baulked by children, dolts and pale memories of ancient warlords? Look at me! Have I aged over the long centuries? Scarcely by a single year, for did I not find elixir, nectar of youth eternal? Never shall my body wither like the brittle leaves of autumn."

Jack of the Hammer gazed almost pitifully at the sorcerer. "Nay, Marek," he said softly, "your body withers not. Instead, it is your mind which has blackened and shrivelled. Once, you were a fine and honourable man, but your very being was twisted by the arts of Darkness and that foul brew from the Pit. Aye, 'twas you who discovered the mixture and nurtured its secrets, but you no longer possess the elixir of life, Marek. It now possesses you!"

"Enough!" roared Pengersek. "By the beard of the Horned One, enough! You dare taunt me, tinner, yet you yourself are no more than a dim memory brought to life by courtesy of a prattling prophecy!"

A flash of hope surged into John's heart. He doesn't know! He doesn't know who Jack really is! He thinks he died centuries ago!"

The sorcerer's boastful tone returned. "Look at me. Gaze upon your Master, for I shall be truly immortal! The secret is mine alone and, with it, the power befitting one who can never die. The work of centuries fulfilled. Now, with the power of this bauble, I shall need the elixir no longer. I shall be Master of the world, of sun and moon, of all Creation. The Abyss shall be no more to me than as a roadside gutter, and the Heaven you speak so highly of shall be but a passing cloud. Both Satanas and your impotent God shall bow down to me.

"And as for your so valiant efforts, they are futile, for is it not written that, on the Eve of Golowan, the powers of warlock, witch and demon cannot stand in the path of a true Mage such as I?"

Jack reached up for his ironstone charm and a spasm of despair flashed across his face. He remembered, it had gone: lost in the bracken and the darkness of the ruined village. John tugged at his sleeve, and there was desperate appeal in his voice. "Jack, is he right?"

"What he says is true," came the resigned answer. "And it is why on only four nights of the year dare he attempt such a spell as this." His voice lowered to a whisper. "And without his ironstone, which is none of the powers in question, even a fallen god stands helpless, let alone a mere craftsman such as I."

The boy opened his mouth to protest, but was stopped. A sudden sonorous note boomed in his ears. None could tell from whence it came, but the sky shuddered to its sound, and the moon turned to blood.

Pengersek's face was a mask of triummph. "The first bell of midnight! The twelfth shall see my work complete and as you stand in helplessness, so shall you witness the coronation of Creation's new master!" His finger pointed downward at Penny's motionless form and the half-hidden Crownstone.

"No!" yelled John, leaping from his pony. The sorcerer raised a hand, calmly and deliberately. Something crashed into the boy's midriff; some unseen force which hurled him, gasping, backwards. He lay in a heap, croaking for breath, but otherwise unhurt for even now, the Crownstone protected the children of Trevelyan. The Witch-Lord shrugged and turned away.

The third bell tolled dolefully and, as its echoes died away, a new sound met their ears. It was an angry noise, somewhere between a roar and a shriek: a drawn-out banshee wail which rose and fell, but always growing louder.

Two brilliant lights glared through the night; huge, frightful eyes rushing up the hill-side towards them. The monster screamed with fury and horses whinnied in terror, their riders fighting furiously for control.

The fifth bell rang.

Calm amid the confusion, the Lord of Pengersek curled his fists into down-turned horns, little and index fingers outstretched. Thin tendrils of the weird, oily smoke began to detach themselves from the column which twisted sluggishly into the sky, and coiled themselves like serpents around the unwinking facets of the Crownstone of Lyonesse.

The air thrummed to the note of the sixth bell, and to a terrible, rending screech. Metal slammed on metal, and a second tall figure suddenly appeared on the capstone of Chûn Quoit . . .

The burly figure of Ben Trevelyan.

22: ... BUT NOT THE MAN

THE two men on the capstone of Chûn Quoit faced each other in silence across the girl's unmoving body. The reeking column of luminous smoke still spiralled upwards and its glowing colours stained the farmer's face like a grotesque mask.

Pengersek reacted first. With a lightning motion, his clenched hand swept up and opened, palm outward. There was a sound like the beating of leathery wings and streams of darkness flowed from the open hand towards the farmer. John felt his throat tighten with fear.

Ben did not flinch but watched with unnatural calm as the evil stream swerved in mid-flight, sucked down into the innocently gleaming Crownstone, which glowed momentarily. The sorcerer stared incredulously at the farmer, uncertain of his next move. A smile began to spread slowly across Ben's face.

A new light shone up at him as the Crownstone of Lyonesse came to life. From Penny's breast, amidst the noisome smoke, its radiance began to emerge; no longer the emerald glow of the past, but a glorious shining of the purest white, growing steadily brighter and, before its brilliance, the oily smoke faltered and dissolved with a soft and desolate sigh.

Still brighter it grew, but in the brief instant before it grew too bright to look at, John saw a change begin to pass over the figure of his uncle. A beard was forming on the strong jaw and his hair grew longer, held in place by a simple crown, heavily inscribed; but the setting for its green gem was empty. A cloak of the deepest red billowed from his shoulders. In that briefest of seconds, the farmer of St Buryan became transformed to the figure of Trevelyan, last of the Lords of Lyonesse.

All eyes twisted away as the Lyonesse Stone erupted into a mighty, dazzling flare; a new earthbound sun which turned night into blinding day. Faraway crystals of the hill-top crags of Belerion flashed sparkling greetings; the desolate moor gleamed whitely and shadows were bottomless pits.

Brighter and brighter it burned until, in a final surge of awesome power, the Crownstone shattered into a thousand fragments. The Lord of Pengersek, shielding his eyes behind an upraised hand, cried out once, staggered back and toppled, stricken, from the capstone. The moor plunged once again into darkness, lit only by the light of the full moon and the flames of the burning castle.

Torn between the powerful spells of the sorcerer and love for its rightful master, the Lyonesse Stone had destroyed itself, flinging its mighty powers upward and outward, away from the body of the girl, to the four corners of the universe, to be forever lost.

The twelfth and last of the ghostly bells boomed out and died away in shuddering echoes. The sky reeled and the moon danced as Time twisted back on itself for the last time. The massed warriors vanished as though they had never been. Fire no longer flickered from the slumped walls of Chûn Castle and not a trace remained of the battle. The lights of Pendeen sparkled in the distance and the probing beams of several lighthouses swept the distant darkness. John reached hesitantly for the wound inflicted by the spriggan's axe but that, too, had gone and left no trace.

Ben, himself once more, shook his head and blinked as though unsure of where he was. He passed a weary hand across his face and looked blankly at John, Corantyn and Jack who gazed back in a stunned silence. Memory and reason returned and the farmer sank to his knees, gently raising Penny's head and cradling it to his broad chest.

Penny opened her eyes, released at last from the dream-world to which she had been sent by the song-spells of the Witch-Lord. His sorcery bound her no longer, but a brief aftertaste lingered; a vision that was fleeting but which would never leave her memory.

At first she saw, not the face of her uncle looking anxiously down at her, but that of the Lord Trevelyan reborn and, as her eyes wandered, she saw the others as they were in the strange half-world of High and Ancient Magic. Her brother stood armoured and cloaked, and battle-light shone in his eyes. His mailed hands clasped a huge, naked sword inscribed with characters which flowed as if alive along its blade.

His two companions seemed to her to be enveloped in glorious light. Tall and majestic, they looked on her with kindness and love. One was unmistakeably Corantyn Nadelek, fully revealed as the mighty Lord of Elves that he had been in the days when that fair race, the eldest of peoples, had walked the earth in great number: a race now reduced to a few sad refugees in remote hills and trackless wastes, waiting with infinite patience for their time to come again. And in his eyes which she'd thought blank and expressionless, she saw all the sadness of his past, the joy of the present, and hope for the future.

The other was Jack of the Hammer, but only his face and the great hammer were familiar for he appeared to her as his true self: Weland, son of Wade, once the god of blacksmiths and workers of metal; smith to the great Aesir, the ancient gods of Asgard. The bull's hide coat, with its horned hood, was for the moment gone, and his deceptively powerful body was sheathed in robe and mail. The bared arms were tightly muscled and on his head was a great winged helmet.

Now she was aware that soft light radiated from them all, and it seemed to her that she lay, not on the rough granite of an ancient megalith, but on soft, yielding turf beneath tall trees heavy with leaf. Stars danced in the sky and all around were voices singing in that strange tongue which would nevermore be unknown to her. The words that Corantyn had spoken came back to her – Blood of the Half-Elven – and she understood.

The vision lasted but a moment and then, as she became fully awake, she felt the coldness of the granite seeping through her clothing, and shivered. Her companions were once again as she had always known them, the moor shimmered under the light of the moon and the breeze ran cool fingers through her hair.

At the foot of the ancient stones, the Witch-Lord stirred, rising unsteadily to his knees. His eyes were downcast but malice and revenge gleamed beneath the hooded lids. He moved like a striking adder, snatched a wickedly curving dagger from his belt and leapt up to bring the blade down on the girl's helpless body.

There was a sharp, musical sound, like the plucking of a harpstring as the great bow of Corantyn sang once more. The enchanter roared with pain as the slim arrow pinned his hand to the very stone, and the knife dropped from nerveless fingers.

"Catch that, devilskin!" cried Jack, leaping forward, hammer in hand. Kicking the knife away into the bracken, he roughly hauled the Witch-Lord away from the Quoit, tearing the pinioned hand free. Pengersek gasped with pain, but the tinner was ruthless now and devoid of all mercy. He flung the sorcerer to the ground, tugging the jewelled headband and the girdle of power from him. The pentagram was ripped from his neck, thrown down and, with a single blow of the hammer, shattered to fragments. The sherds glowed white with heat for a moment before flying away into the night, hissing and howling. Finally, the golden headband, set with the seven jewels of the seven planets, was hammered into a formless mass, its stone shattered. Wisps of vapour rose from it and were dispersed by the breeze.

Jack turned as he glimpsed a movement from the corner of his eye. There, standing nervously a little way off, was the sorcerer's familiar, the coal-black demon-mare, whose burning eyes glared uncertainly.

"So," murmured the tinner, "you escaped the fate of the hunters. Well, my proud beauty, escape from me!"

The mare kicked up her heels to flee, but the hammer, flung with frightening accuracy, struck her full on the diamond star of her forehead before, astonishingly, flying back through the air and into Jack's waiting hand. As the devil-horse crumpled and fell, so her shape writhed and diminished; shrinking into a grotesque parody of human form. There was the briefest glimpse of horns and clawed hands then, finally, it became a black serpent which slunk away into the heather, never to be seen again.

Jack glowered down at the sorcerer, helpless now without his trappings of power. His fear-filled eyes stared with disbelief at the tinner and at the great hammer in his hand.

"That which Mjöllnir, hammer of Thor, could achieve," said Jack, "so too can this. Behold, Pengersek: behold the hammer of Weland the Smith, cast in the same mould, fashioned by the same hand.

"Ah, Marek; centuries ago I faced and defeated you and you have thought me long dead. Know to your everlasting sorrow that I am neither mortal, nor the devil you once thought me. Know you now that I am Weland, son of Wade, god of the Aesir, and I shall walk the earth in mortal form until the Aesir rise again."

Pengersek said nothing. He seemed changed from a tall and handsome man into an old, withered wretch, huddling tight against the stones of Chûn Quoit as though seeking refuge in their agelessness.

Ben Trevelyan lifted his niece from the capstone and led her to her friends. This time, he looked deep into the eyes of Corantyn without fear or distrust, and grasped his hand in silent gratitude. Jack he regarded almost with reverence and nodded his thanks before clasping John in a bear-like hug.

Out to sea, invisible from the hill, there sailed a black ship. Its sombre sails cracked and billowed and the bows crashed through the foam, making rapid way against both wind and tide. So close did it come beneath Portheras Cliff that only its topmasts were visible from the land, but the iron coast was no barrier for such a ship as this. The whole ominous vessel forsook the waves, rising to glide overland, across the sand and boulders and up the ravine-like valley, its course set for Chûn.

Through the night spoke a voice, great and dark:

> "THE HOUR IS COME, BUT NOT THE MAN!"
> "THE HOUR IS COME, BUT NOT THE MAN!"
> "THE HOUR IS COME, BUT NOT THE MAN!"

The sorcerer wailed in terror. He twisted and turned, grovelling in the dust, frantically, hopelessly, seeking a way of escape.

The dark ship, with its bulging sails, changed its shape to become part of a dense cloud rushing in on Chûn, on the wings of a wind which threatened to pluck the onlookers from the hill. The cloud spread huge, leathery wings, black against the moonlit sky, and folded them again before growing suddenly smaller, collapsing in on itself to form a black, whirling funnel, hovering menacingly above the capstone of Chûn Quoit. It corkscrewed downward, shrinking as though being sucked into the great slab.

"Turn your backs!" commanded Jack sharply. "If you would keep your sanity!" His words demanded instant obedience, but he himself was unafraid and he alone faced the Quoit.

A young man sat on the capstone of the megalith, idly dangling his legs over the edge. His skin was of a coppery hue and his expression was one of sardonic amusement. His hair was dark and tightly curled, while his eyes, upturned at the corners, added a lightly mocking tone to his features.

"My greetings to you, Weland." The voice was light and pleasant, while the arms swept wide in an exaggerated, almost derisive, movement.

"And mine to you, Satanas," replied Jack guardedly. His eyes held the other's gaze. "These four are under my protection. I charge thee: take only what is thine."

The Dark Prince shrugged his shoulders and smiled, without malice. "You need not fear, son of Wade. I call for one; I shall take but one. I have no quarrel with you or your company; indeed, your victory has been to the benefit of us all."

Jack inclined his head in query, and the youthful figure explained. "Should Marek have succeeded this night, he would have posed much more than a threat. Not only would I have been in peril; your own clan of Asgard would never more have risen. Even the Christos and His Father would have been sorely threatened."

He gazed down at the sorcerer who lay as rigid and immobile as a fallen statue, eyes staring sightlessly at a universe that had been so nearly his, and would now be forever beyond his reach.

"His power has fled and his soul is mine. He sold it to me centuries ago in the mountains of the Saracens where he learned his art, and the debt is long overdue. He was clever and cunning:

he cheated me once, even eluding my searches, but one cannot doubt his courage. He knew well the risk of returning to his native soil; perhaps the greatest gamble of all history. Consider the stakes: his soul, or the Universe.

"But this he failed to grasp. The Universe is subject to laws of its own making, which we must observe, or perish. There must be balance. Good and evil must co-exist, and be equal.

"Marek would have swayed that balance. A new power such as his would surely have upset the equilibrium, and the Universe itself might finally have collapsed."

"Would Marek truly have become such a power?" said Jack, coolly. "If you had such concern, why did you not aid us? Am I to believe that he could have evaded you for so long, or was it that he was here to do your bidding and failed? Perhaps we will never know the truth, for it is well said, Satanas, that you are the Lord of Liars."

The Dark One laughed mockingly as dark vapours began to swirl around his figure, hiding it from sight as they thickened, growing black and monstrous. They devoured the ancient megalith and the stricken figure at its base, spreading rapidly to engulf the entire hill. Thunder growled in the midst of the murk, and a sudden blast of wind shrieked across the hill-top, with a strength that would force even a god to stagger.

The moon was blotted out, and howling darkness fell, but Corantyn and the three Trevelyans stood, firm and defiant, under the protection of Weland the Smith. In the raging gloom were voices, lost and soulless, then both wind and darkness left them once more under the eye of the midsummer moon.

The sorcerer had gone and retreating into the west was the great cloud which, for a moment, raised itself up, rearing high above them like a towering blade, poised to strike. Then, in the face of a fresh, southerly breeze, it shuddered, dissolved and faded to nothing.